To the City

Gillian Tindall

HUTCHINSON
London Melbourne Auckland Johannesburg

This edition first published in 1987 by Hutchinson, an imprint of
Century Hutchinson Ltd, Brookmount House, 62–65 Chandos Place,
London WC2N 4NW

Century Hutchinson South Africa (Pty) Ltd
PO Box 337, Berglvei, 2012 South Africa

Century Hutchinson Australia Pty Ltd
PO Box 496, 16–22 Church Street, Hawthorn, Victoria 3122, Australia

Century Hutchinson New Zealand Ltd
PO Box 40–086, Glenfield, Auckland 10, New Zealand

Set 11/13 Bembo Input Typesetting, London.
Printed and Bound in Great Britain by
Anchor Brendon Limited, Tiptree, Essex

British Library Cataloguing in Publication Data

Tindall, Gillian
  To the city.
  I. Title
  823'.914[F]   PR6070.145
ISBN 0–09–170540.1

To the City

This book is dedicated to
T. R. ('Tosco') Fyvel
1907–1985
in grateful and affectionate memory

Author's Note

Readers who know Vienna well may wonder why I have made the Prater wheel function at New Year, a time when it is usually closed, and have shifted the Rathaus Christmas Fair to the foot of it. The answer is that, since this is not a work of documentary fact but of imagination, minor liberties have been taken with space and time in an otherwise real city.

Gillian Tindall

1

'Lemmings', he wrote in his Notebook. He looked at it a moment and underlined it: *Lemmings*. Then he began to write fast, copying from the typescript of a book on myths he was editing.

The Lemming has become popular as a metaphoric figure for the supposedly heedless, self-destructive urges among humankind. There must by now be several hundred thousand printed references to the 'lemming-like' behaviour of the nuclear powers and their arms-race.

However it is possible that we have misunderstood the lemming and that his behaviour does have a rationale, albeit one unsuited to the circumstances in which he currently exists. The theory that the lemming is in fact seeking, not death, but an extension of life in a far-off place known to his ancestors, is undoubtedly appealing and has gained a certain mythic currency. At least one poet (John Masefield) has enshrined it in verse:

> *Once, it is thought, there was a westward land*
> *(Now drowned) where there was food for those starved things,*
> *And memory of the place has burnt its brand*
> *In the little brains of all the Lemming-kings.*
> *. . . Perhaps long since there was a land beyond,*
> *Westwards from death, some city, some calm place*
> *Where one could taste God's quiet and be fond*
> *With the little beauty of a human face:*
> *But now the land is drowned. Yet still we press*
> *Westward in search, to death, to nothingness.*

He read it through, then thought a minute. Something bothered him: why 'westwards', specifically? Why not 'eastwards'? Simply because that was the way the sun moved and therefore time should move that way? Oh well. It was only a poem.

He drew a neat line under it and laid his Notebook aside.

Only a poem. But his Notebook was filling up with them.

When he had begun keeping his Notebook nine months before, in stealth and anxiety as if it represented some private, slightly shameful vice, he had not realized how much good and even bad poetry would speak to his particular need. '*Nothing so sharply reminds a man he is mortal . . .*' That had been the first one, memorized hastily from a book picked up at random in someone else's bathroom, later quarried out of an anthology. And after that there had been many, many more. Prose passages too, but these tended to be more didactic, less crucial. Poems, it seemed, were the pegs on which the web of his Notebook was strung.

As a boy and young man, though addicted to novels, he had largely missed poetry. He thought that he must have been too hasty for it then, over-articulate himself and too consciously rational. Was it abnormal to take to it in middle age, seeking belatedly in its brevities and metaphors the key to something only half-perceived?

Other men's lines. Wrested from their contexts. He was well aware of the questionable value of such scissors-and-paste work. But this, at the moment, seemed his only way of codifying his own experience, of making any sense of it. His testimony. Other men's lines. But he was, after all, an editor by trade. And in his more optimistic moments he even dared hope that some pattern of lines, an eventual pattern of meaning, would emerge.

Anyway, he liked the lemming passage for its own sake. With a small but distinct sense of satisfaction he read it through again. Then he closed the Notebook and stowed it in its place in his jacket pocket.

The untidy pile of typescript in front of him was only half read and would need a good deal doing to it, but the day was ending. His office, and the rooms beyond, were silent. The one or two other people who had slipped in earlier, on this unofficial day, had gone home. There was probably no one now in the high Covent Garden building but himself and the caretaker.

Telling himself he should be savouring the solitude, for there would be little of it for the next week, he wrote a

2

lengthy memo for his secretary to find on Monday, and left it on top of the typescript weighted down with a soapstone beaver his daughter had given him when she was twelve. (What did a lemming look like? He must find out.)

Just before he left he decided to make another phone call.

The number rang and was eventually answered, but not by the person he wanted.

'Naomi? Joe here. Sorry if I dragged you away from something . . . Have you got Ted there?'

Ted, however, was out at a meeting.

'No, nothing important. I'm off tomorrow for a week's holiday . . . Yes, skiing. I just wanted to wish him Happy New Year before I left. And you, of course. You'll tell him I rang?'

Naomi was Ted's daughter. Although she had taken so long to answer the phone, she seemed inclined now to detain Joe in conversation. Patiently, he detached her, and rang off.

He sat again another long minute, battling with a desire to ring another number, draw another woman from her kitchen. But it would be no use. He had spoken to her already.

He quashed his yearning, got up and left the building, locking the street door behind him. The noise of its closing resounded in the darkened stairwell behind, as if signalling a long absence. He felt guilt, as if abandoning something. Silly, he told himself; he would be back again in less than two weeks.

Once outside in the street he felt better. Although it was just after Christmas, Charing Cross tube station, when he reached it, was thick with people; vaguely festive and disoriented, clutching bags proclaiming sales. It was evident from the clogging crowds on the escalators that the situation must be worse down on the platforms. Why did people continue to descend into an area that was clearly over-full already? An announcement being made was too garbled to be understood, but the notice on a blackboard was clear. With the usual formula it regretted any inconvenience to passengers: there were delays to all Northern Line destinations. The cause, it said with precise inadequacy, was 'a person under a train'.

He decided to walk up to Tottenham Court Road or maybe Warren Street. By the time he got there the lemming might be removed, the trains running again. He felt quite peaceful now, out in the evening city. He would be glad of a walk. The poor lemming was nothing to do with him: he managed to forget him again.

Nothing so sharply reminds a man he is mortal
As leaving a place . . .

The lines were in his mind again the following morning, as he manoeuvred the car into a place in the long-term car park at Gatwick. There was frost on the ground and perhaps ice. The sky was still uncompromisingly dark. These skiing trips – in which he rejoiced, for which he yearned months ahead in the clammy greyness of the British autumn – always, he thought, seemed to start at such a traumatically early hour, thereby introducing tension and foreboding into what should have been entire pleasure. Fear in the heart: known in another language as *angst*.

Oh rubbish. They had got up at a quarter to four after a few brief tense hours of sleep, had done last-minute things with suitcases, keys and heating systems, had driven across London's lighted night-time wastes and out of it into the deeper night – what was wrong with him was probably nothing more interesting than low blood sugar.

To reassure himself as much as his wife, he said aloud:

'As soon as we've checked in the cases and found the Lovells we'll have a cup of coffee.'

'If we've got time.' Caroline's voice was preoccupied, her head turned from him as she put on her down mitts. The familiar irritation rose within him.

'Of course we've got time. The plane doesn't leave till six-forty. As usual, we've allowed ourselves too much time, if anything. Why shouldn't there be time for coffee?'

4

'We've got to find the Lovells, haven't we? And the children too, remember.' The same preoccupied, deflating tone.

'How can we not find the Lovells? And as for the children, you know perfectly well they've got their own tickets. It's up to them to find us.'

All right, all right. I'm worried too that that optimistic trio in a rattling old Mini will not have allowed enough time and now, even now, will be driving too fast down the night roads . . . *But why must you be so bloody dreary about it?*

In silence, but methodically, they extracted the cases and bags from the boot. Years of family experience had taught them a routine together, and had taught Joe that suggestions about travelling light this time were, with Caroline, fruitless. Always – always, always – she brought with them what seemed to Joe too much luggage. It was unfailingly well-packed, well-organized; folded clothes inter-layered with tissue paper, socks padding edges, bottles and jars safe in plastic bags. But there was just too much of it. She seemed unable to think of travelling in any other way. He had tried telling himself that it was all part of her being a Good Wife, remembering to bring things that feckless husbands, children and friends forgot: she was also the one with Paracetamol, with spare socks or jerseys to lend, with more books for the bored, with the Scrabble set, the pack of cards, the only hair-drier . . . He had also tried telling himself, recently, that some buried fear of her own expressed itself in this over-provisioning just as his did in – other ways. Both these views of Caroline's luggage were no doubt valid. But the sheer volume and weight of it continued to goad him.

Why should two adults of normal strength set off *anywhere*, let alone for a mere week's skiing, with more cases between them than they could physically manage to carry? *Insane, insane* cried his mind darkly, as he began to ferry the cases in relays to the nearest stop for the Terminal shuttle-bus.

'He refuses to organize *anything* in advance – and then we end up with this extraordinary collection of *things*, like rich

5

refugees.' It was not Caroline's voice but Mary Lovell's, loud and cheerful, joking at the expense of her equally cheerful husband, Tom. A large couple in several senses, they and their possessions seemed like a benign invasion in the warm, lighted Terminal. Tom had skis with him, as did Joe, but he also seemed to be hung about like a pedlar with extra boots, coats and plastic bags. Mary, her shaggy fur coat open, handbag and shoulder bag dangling, bore in her arms like a baby a large parcel which Joe recognized as containing books.

'Brought your latest to sell to the Austrians, dear?'

Mary rolled her eyes at him behind her horn-rimmed glasses.

'Enough of your cheek. This is homework. Books I'm judging for some prize. The bastards promised them for me before Christmas, but they only turned up yesterday.'

'Stuck in the Christmas time-warp.'

'Expect so. *Not* that I would have had time to read them over Christmas, as it turned out. I don't know why I fondly imagine, each year, that I'll have *time*, warped or otherwise, over Christmas.'

Mary wrote children's fiction, successfully. Several of her books for younger children had been published by Joe's firm, though he himself was concerned mainly with educational books. He had known Mary a long time, even longer – he suddenly thought now, seeing her in the Terminal – than he had known Caroline: he and Mary had been at Oxford together. Now he said to her:

'Well, I don't know why you imagine you'll have time to read that pile on a skiing holiday either. I think you've just brought them to show off and to make Tom and me feel unintellectual.' And Caroline, and Caroline.

'Rubbish. Or rather – have it your own way. I shall shut myself away in the bedroom and develop theories while you lot are quarrelling over Scrabble in the bar.'

'You won't,' he said with conviction. 'You know you've often said you like skiing because it switches your head off.

6

So do I. It's Time Out, skiing is – like Christmas. We're extending Christmas, going now, immediately afterwards.'

And we are avoiding the more equivocal echoes produced by the New Year at home, and the first empty, uncertain days of January. Another poem nagged in his retentive memory – had been nagging for days, in the brief, dark spaces between the candlelit parties with friends and neighbours, in the cold mornings when his children now slept late and he was the one to wake with the dawn:

> *For now the time of gifts is gone –*
> *O boys that grow, O snows that melt;*
> *O bathos that the years must fill –*

'O boys that grow'. And girls too. Jennifer was twenty-one now, David nineteen. Tom and Mary's Jerome was twenty. Never again would Christmas be magic to them.

Not that this Christmas had been unsuccessful. Jennifer and David had both been at home for it and had participated loyally in the celebrations. But their very willingness to do so, he knew with a sudden pang, showed that they were now indisputably grown-up. They too were prepared, like their parents and their parents' friends, to suspend time and judgement in the unreal days of the holiday, to renew love, to ignore feuds – prepared because they were well aware of real time ticking on, and on, irrevocably carrying them away from childhood, from their parents, from all that had not only sheltered them but had been there for that purpose and arguably was now redundant. This Christmas, the house of childhood, like a great tithe barn, had been briefly swept, lighted, garnished with wreaths and oranges and lanterns. But now Christmas was past and it would stand empty again.

In fact two days earlier David had set off on an odyssey that (Joe understood) involved calling on the Lovells in Hertfordshire, driving in Jerome Lovell's Mini to stay near Leicester with Lisette, David's girlfriend, and then the three of them driving all the way down to Gatwick in the small hours of the present morning. In vain had Joe and Caroline inquired why Jerome couldn't accompany his own parents to the airport, and why Lisette couldn't stay the night in London so that she, David, Joe and Caroline could all drive down in one (safer) car?

'I told you, Dad, there's this party Lisette's cousin is giving . . .' Vague and unanswerable.

'It isn't that at all really, of course,' Mary Lovell had said crisply over the phone to Joe. 'It's much more that they *like* making these dottily inconvenient arrangements which involve long, unnecessary journeys and no one getting enough sleep. Since Tom gave Jerome the money to buy that Mini – not that we could have stopped him, he was hell bent on getting a car anyway – he's been popping around all over England. Extraordinary. In our day surely once one was at Oxford one *stayed* there for the term. Wasn't there even some rule about it?'

Jerome was at Oxford; David, and Lisette, were at York.

'I think,' said Joe, 'there's some further wild justification for bringing an extra car to Gatwick. Something to do with Jerome driving David and Lisette back to York afterwards and staying up there for a couple of days.'

'Straight up to York? Oh really! But David will have to come back home first to collect all his stuff. Won't he?'

'So I should imagine. I suspect in fact we'll be harbouring your Jerome for several days at least before David gets himself sorted out. Like his mother, he always has mounds of belongings.' The prospect of Jerome sleeping on a camp bed again in David's room, as when they were little boys, filled him with a febrile happiness. And there would be Lisette as well . . . But no, in that case Jerome would have to sleep somewhere else, wouldn't he? In Jennifer's by-then empty room, perhaps.

And what was Caroline's attitude going to be at the prospect of David and his beloved sleeping together under their roof? Caroline had several times in the safer past intimated that she didn't really think it 'helpful' or 'a good thing' for parents to be so overtly accommodating, regardless of what 'went on' elsewhere.

Not helpful . . . not a good thing: the circumlocutions used today by the natural Puritan who knows that the words she really means ('immoral' and 'wanton') are taboo. These days, Caroline, in her capacity as voluntary social worker and justice of the peace, was adept at such circumlocutions.

But she was not worrying about that now, this morning, as the Beeches and the Lovells finally rid themselves of the heavier part of their belongings at the check-in desk and made their way upstairs to the café. She was worrying that David (and Jerome and Lisette too, of course) were lying in blood and twisted metal by the side of some dark road. Not of course that she used such alarming words, confining herself to wondering if anything could have 'happened' to the children, but on her lips the verb was laden with fear. Since Mary, Tom and Joe himself all shared this anxiety secretly to some extent, they were determinedly brisk with Caroline.

'They'll turn up,' said Tom shortly. 'They wouldn't miss this plane. They know when they're on to a good thing – like parents paying for an entire skiing holiday, near enough, for the pleasure of their company.' Tom meant, no doubt, to sound jovial, but in fact his remarks came out disagreeably cynical. Joe reflected, not for the first time in Tom's company, that those who prosper to the point of becoming rich often seem to need to make calculating remarks rather than generous ones, and to impute calculation to others. Effect of wealth? Or its hidden cause? Tom was 'in' electronics, and Joe knew little about that field though was increasingly aware that he ought to. Word processors and so forth. New printing methods, storage on floppy disks, bind-in facility . . . No, dammit, he was going to ski this week, not speculate on the future of his own trade.

As if realizing that his remark may have sounded uncharitable, Tom said breezily:

'Right – brekkers. First brekkers, anyway. What are we all having? Coffee? Buns? Don't know what else they run to at this hour.' The café indeed was nearly deserted, with one brown-skinned woman drooping behind the urn and a darker male pushing a mop slowly between the yellow plastic tables. Round one table a large, Middle Eastern-looking family with many children and plastic bags murmured to each other.

'No other skiers,' said Caroline looking round anxiously. 'I hope,' she added, with an attempt at a joke, 'we've come to the right place.'

'We're *early*,' Joe could not stop himself saying. 'Really early. You saw there was hardly anyone checking in for our flight yet. And that's why the children aren't here yet either.' *So for God's sake shut up about them.*

'Just coffee for me,' said Mary, showing her generation by peering into the mirror of a powder compact. 'My stomach hasn't woken up properly yet.'

Inexorably, however, as it seemed, the four of them returned to the theme of the absent children.

'Shame Jenn couldn't come,' said Tom. He had always been fond of Jennifer, seeing in her, Joe thought, the daughter he and Mary had never had.

'Yes, rather a shame,' Joe hesitated. 'But she's very wrapped up in her job. She's only had it a few months, of course, hasn't amassed much leave-entitlement yet. And you know, Tom, she's never been that keen on skiing, not like the boys.' Like her mother. But I won't say that.

'Pity, all the same,' said Tom sentimentally. He asked, after a pause – 'This job she's gone into – hospital adminis-tration: she likes it? It's what she really wants to do?'

'So it seems,' said Joe firmly. Yes, I too have a faint pain in my heart about my Jenn, so good, so nice but – no, not as pretty as she promised to be in childhood, and a worrier, too painstaking: not at ease in life as her brother is. And not sexy. But let's not go into that now, for God's sake.

Mary was saying cheerfully to Caroline:

'Let's see, how many rooms have we got between us in this chalet we're going to? Yes, I know you sent me all the details, dear, when I sent you our cheque, but what with

Christmas things like that seem to have silted down beneath a deep litter of goose-grease and used glasses . . . Well: one room for us, I suppose, one for you and Joe, and – what? A double and a single for the kids? Or do they all muck in together still or does one of them share with a stranger, or what?'

She turned her head from Caroline to light the first of her many daily cigarettes, and, as she did so, Joe caught an amused gleam behind her glasses which he rather thought was directed at him. As so often Mary's prattle was not as ingenuous as it sounded. Very likely she was aware of Caroline's suppressed tension on these matters and was trying to see the lie of the land before the children were actually there. To forestall Caroline, Joe said quickly:

'We asked initially for two doubles for the kids, so now they can sort themselves out as they want.'

'But,' put in Caroline, 'the chalet company have said that if we don't want the fourth bed they might have another customer for it – save us the money, you see, and accommodate someone who otherwise wouldn't get in. They've made an over-booking muddle on one of their other chalets, I got the impression.'

'Yes, but what permutation?' persisted Mary naughtily. 'I mean – forgive my crudity, everyone; it's too early in the morning for tact. Do Jerome and David share and Lisette go in with a Lady Unknown? Or – what?' She had been going to spell out the other alternative, Joe knew, but backed down at the last moment because of Caroline's expression. Caroline said quickly:

'Well I should think so, since the other bed was originally for Jennifer. I mean, when we asked for two more doubles we thought she might be coming.'

'Oh, was that a possibility?' said Tom, waking up at Jennifer's name. Not apparently noticing any constraint in the conversation, he went on:

'I thought it was Anna who might've been going to join us at one time. You know – Anna Morley. Wasn't there a theory she might come with us, as Aiden doesn't ski?'

Anna Morley had also been at Oxford with Mary and Joe.

Into the tiny pool of silence and restraint that settled round Anna's dropped name, Mary quickly plunged. Mischievous instigator of this conversation, thought Joe, she was also its saviour. Typical.

'Oh? I thought that idea never really got off the ground. Or is it still a possibility she might turn up? I mean, she'd fly direct from Manchester, wouldn't she?'

Joe said he didn't know. Mary hastened on:

'Oh well, if she should appear she'd have to share with Lisette, of course, but if she's not likely to it seems a bit academic and we're left with our genteel dilemma, are we not? Dears, if it makes the slightest difference may I lay my own cards on the table? Neither Tom nor I will think it *a bit* odd or shocking or unsuitable or any of those things – will we, Tom? – if Jerome ends up as the odd one out in this bedroom allocation. Apart from anything else, it might even open new vistas to him! I mean, to date he never seems fully aware of such matters at all, and I find myself quite wishing he *would* get off with some accommodating chalet girl in self-defence. So far all his passion seems to be directed towards his car, and producing abstruse plays translated from Serbo-Croat in damp college gardens.'

'Producing them rather superbly, you must admit,' said Joe, grateful for the rescue into the subject of Jerome.

'Well, I suppose so. But I must confess that my heart *quails* rather when I know it's our duty to go and sit through another one.'

'And my bottom quails,' said Tom coarsely. 'Sitting on a cold bench with my particular Old Trouble is not my idea of a treat.'

'Of course it's not a treat, you booby, it's parental duty. Oh Joe – Caroline – he *was* so pleased that you turned up to the last one, though. It's *well* beyond the call of duty that you should go slogging off to Oxford for that. And bringing that *Spectator* man with you: he wrote such a nice piece. Jerome was thrilled.'

Caroline said firmly, 'Oh we enjoyed it, we really did. Didn't we, Joe?'

Did we? thought Joe, rummaging in memory, I've no idea. No idea, that is, whether I enjoyed the production for its own sake, I don't remember much about it. No, what I remember enjoying was just being there and seeing that Jerome was doing what he wanted to do and being applauded for it. Because Jerome is more than a friendly, talented boy to me, more than the son of old friends: I count him mentally as a member of my extended family. (What family?)

I don't think Caroline feels this way. She doesn't need to, perhaps. But David does. Only this Christmas he and I were talking about Jerome, and David said, 'Yes, of course I'm glad Jerome's coming skiing too. I mean, I'm always pleased to see old Jerome, I never think "Do I want to?" particularly. I've known him since ever. He's more like a cousin to Jenn and me, isn't he?'

David had been born gregarious, more so than his sister, had grown into a little boy and then a larger boy who thrived on having people round him. He was, it seemed, a member of a big family by nature, though not in fact. There were some real cousins, on Caroline's side, but they led an alien life in Shropshire and Caroline herself had never cultivated them much.

At this conversation with David, Joe, as so often before, had reflected briefly, poignantly and without conclusion on the many cousins his son would have had if history had gone differently.

Then all at once, looking unnaturally large, healthy and real in the half-lit cafeteria, the three grown children were there before them, stamping feet in coloured boots, kissing the mothers, wanting coffee – or milk – or anything – accusing the grown ups of being irresponsibly hard to find.

The ski holiday had officially begun.

Joe had been looking forward to this departure for months, for several separate reasons. But as he and his companions were actually shuffling in a queue in the departure lounge, boarding cards in hand, he felt his familiar panic gripping him.

Some years earlier, before this nuisance had got so bad, he had convinced himself that what he suffered from was fear of flying, a commonplace and apparently respectable syndrome. He had even discussed it in these terms with acquaintances who claimed a similarly labelled disability, swapping symptoms and tranquillizers as if the ailment was low back pain, or the chronic cystitis about which Caroline carried on a heartfelt correspondence with one or two women friends. But he had insidiously come to realize that, for him, aeroplanes were really neither here nor there; they merely happened to be the medium via which, today, most significant journeys were effected. The same sense of irrational fear and despair could be produced in him by boarding a long distance train, especially one where he must sleep overnight, as if the claustrophobic hours stretched out on a bunk put an impassable barrier between one life and another. Another life? No, no, it was rather death that he feared lay waiting for him beyond the sky, beyond the night train. Or, if not final death itself, then a rehearsal for death:

> Nothing so sharply reminds a man he is mortal
> As leaving a place
> In a winter morning's dark, the air on his face
> Unkind as the touch of sweating metal
> Simple goodbyes to children or friends become
> A felon's numb
> Farewell . . .

Rubbish, all rubbish of course – in this instance. He was not leaving his children or his closest friends but taking them with him in a protective Mafia. Maudlin, self-indulgent rot. Now, what was this seat-number . . .

Oh God, don't let *this* plane be the one that, by tomorrow's grey dawn, is a grey, unclear photograph of smoking remains on the front page of every newspaper. Oh God, who cannot undo the past (they say), undo the future that

14

is there, kindly amending your Plan while there is still time.
There's a good, senile old chap.

God wot rot – a favourite phrase of Jerome's when, at the
age of about fifteen he had, as his mother said, Become
Intellectual. Now about this bag . . . Most of the lockers
full already, of course. No, Caroline seemed to have
commandeered an empty one. At her suggestion he handed
his heavy jacket thankfully to her.

– But, after all, there was no mystery in his feeling, merely
a lack of applied common sense; for it was classic, wasn't it,
the journey as a metaphor for death? It was the stuff of
innumerable cults and legends. As he settled himself into his
seat he earnestly tried to apply intellect and culture if he
could not apply sense, summoning up to reassure himself
Ships of the Dead, the Isles of the Blessed and all the other
archetypes. The ancient Egyptians used to provide their
distinguished dead with everything they would need for a
great trek up the Nile, including bearers and pack-animals
all miniaturized in clay. The Chinese to this day equip their
departed – ah, 'departed', the very word expresses the
journey – with horses, food and cars, all made out of paper,
which are ceremonially burnt. What it is to be an educational
publisher with a ragbag memory.

Recently, checking sources for a social history of the Great
War, he had bethought himself to look up for the first time
the origin of the title *Journey's End*. Happily embroiled in
the *Oxford Dictionary of Quotations*, he found the source was
apparently Dryden:

Life's but an inn upon the road
And death the journey's end.

But he was intrigued to realize, browsing down the page,
that a phrase that was the same to the ear cropped up in
quite another context:

Journeys end in lovers' meetings
Every wise man's son doth know.

Ho, hum. Had that become part of his personal journey-
angst too? Death and Love as twin, conflated destinations?

Coming, coming . . . Another classic. To the passionate Elizabethans 'to die' was a synonym for sexual release.

It's a long, long trail a-winding . . .

And then, yesterday afternoon, when he had been in the office trying to polish off various bits of work left over from before Christmas, already feeling his journey-angst cooking up inside him like an impending physical illness, the phone had rung and it had been Anna.

'Where are you ringing from?' A convincing image of her already in London assailed him.

'Manchester. Where else?'

'I don't know, I just thought . . . Well?'

'Look, Joe. I don't think I *can* come.'

'We've been into all that – ' He felt suddenly exhausted.

'You don't understand. Aidan's got flu.'

There was a pause, during which Joe essayed the image of Aidan, whom he always thought of as armoured in dark clothes, red-eyed in rumpled pyjamas like a giant cross child. Then he said angrily:

'But that's not the point, is it?'

'It happens to be absolutely true.'

'But if it hadn't been Aidan with flu it'd've been something else, wouldn't it? You never meant to come skiing anyway.'

'Well . . . As you say, we've been into all that. It's just that when I came to think it over it didn't seem a terribly good idea.' Not one for over-articulating ideas anyway, Anna on the telephone was at her most elusive and infuriating.

He said helplessly:

'But you've come with us all before, twice. Years ago. That time in Meribel when we taught the children to ski. It was all such fun.'

'Quite. Years ago.'

'It doesn't make any difference. It needn't . . .' Oh, let us get back, back to that innocence, back into that Garden of Eden (as it now seems) when there was no scheming, no guilt, no fear, when all was implicit and therefore still whole: an intimation only, a half-formed dream, a vague promise

16

in a future that still seemed full of unknown but benign things. Back to the unreachable past.

'Look,' she said abruptly, an obscure alarm in her voice, 'I've got to ring off.'

'But our other agreement still holds,' he said sharply, trying to keep the sense of a question out of his voice.

'Yes, yes,' she said quickly, 'that still holds.'

'But if Aidan has flu . . . ?'

'He'll be over it by then,' she said. Then the line went dead.

That had been yesterday afternoon.

It was after that, pushing aside the other papers he would not now deal with until his return, that he had copied into his Notebook the passage about lemmings, and tried to phone an old friend.

They were settled into their seats now, in the inevitable pairs, except for Jerome.

'Maybe I'll change places with Jerome by and by so that he can sit by you,' murmured Caroline. 'We don't want him to feel left out, do we?'

'Good idea – but I'm hoping to sleep for a bit first.' No, dear, we don't want him to feel left out. We don't want anyone to feel left out, including you. Impossible equations.

The engines were revving. His heart seemed to be swelling inside him. Sweat crept on his skin under layers of clothes, like small insects. He had already taken (these days such was his strategy) two tranquillizers wheedled from a doctor friend: pride and secrecy created a powerful resistance in him to going and asking his own GP for such a thing.

With the pills' aid he presently dozed. At least, he realized after a long space of engine noise and timelessness, that he must have done so, for he had been walking round a name-less foreign city in the half-light, where snow lay white in the runnels of cobbles and the corners of ancient buildings more substantial than those in British towns. He went swiftly, dream-walking with no effort, for he was going to meet someone in a dark hotel. But which hotel, which, among all these high dwellings? And then maybe it was not an hotel after all, where she would be waiting for him but (of course) his aunt and uncle's large house out at Turkenshanzplatz, so the city was not nameless and there she would be . . . But Turkenshanzplatz was a long tram-ride distant, and time was growing short; his automatic happiness was being fast overtaken by dread. He woke, and a tepid relief invaded him.

Day, and even bright sunlight had come. They must be above the clouds. Toy breakfasts were being brought round on film-wrapped trays.

He realized presently that other things had changed while he had been in that dark city. Mary Lovell was now sitting beside him; Caroline and Tom seemed to be doing *The Times* crossword together in the seat behind. Across the aisle David and Lisette were plugged into one Walkman tape recorder, like Siamese twins sharing a vital organ, but while David was dreamily beating time to a faintly perceptible tinny vibration, Lisette appeared to have retreated into sleep like a baby in its pram, dark lashes on curve of cheek. Evidently the purpose of changing places to sit with Jerome had not materialized; craning round, Joe located him a little further up the gangway, reading with the rapt, nervous attention that was habitual with him. Joe settled back into his own seat, satisfied now that none of his tribe was mysteriously missing. Almost at once Jerome banged his book shut and said loudly, 'God wot rot!'

'What rot is it this time?' Mary asked her son with mild amusement, craning round to look at him in her turn.

'That Marguerite Duras novel that won a Goncourt. I ask you – look at the last para. You couldn't get away with such vapid pretension in English.' And he unfolded his gangling body to lean over seat-backs and precipitate the thin, paperbound book into Mary's lap. She opened it obediently, and Joe read silently over her shoulder:

'. . . Il lui avait dit que c'était comme avant, qu'il l'aimait encore, qu'il ne pourrait jamais cesser de l'aimer, qu'il l'aimerait jusqu'à sa mort.'

' . . . that he could never stop loving her, that he would love her until his death.'

After a more laboured pause for translation, Mary said, with a snort that resembled her son's, 'Pure Barbara Cartland.'

'Mmm, pretty feeble in English,' Joe agreed. But thought, *And yet, and yet* – He tried it to himself in German: 'Dass er niemals aufhören könne sie zu lieben, dass er sie lieben würde bis zu seinem Tode.' But in that language it took on a high-flown unreality like a Schubert *Lied*. Unwilling to explore the matter further for the moment, though in his livelier moods the differing personalities of languages was of an unfailing interest to him, he got up to return the book to Jerome – who was already selecting another one from a well-stocked bag – and came back to sit heavily beside Mary. Feeling her eyeing him, he said abruptly:

'I wish I didn't hate travelling so.'

'Still?' Carefully neutral, sympathetic tone. He and she had discussed this before: indeed he thought he remembered now that it had been she who had first suggested that perhaps it was not really aeroplanes he hated but journeys in general.

'Still. Worse, if anything.'

'But you love it when you get there.'

'I know. That's why it's so stupid. It's as if the whole thing means too much to me all round.'

'It's not stupid,' she said, still in the same dispassionate-friend tone that rather annoyed him, so that he half wished he had not started this. 'I thought about it after you and I had talked, that other time, and it came to me: I mean, surely it's quite obvious and understandable really, even if it isn't strictly rational?'

He raised one eyebrow to allow her to continue, and she said.

'How old were you when you first came to England?'

'Seven. Coming eight.'

'That's about what I thought. It's awfully young. And yet old enough to retain a lot from before. "Give me a child until it is seven" etc . . . Surely your fear of journeys is all

19

about that one-way journey you did then. It must have been
– well, traumatic is the classic word, isn't it?'

He said grumpily, deliberately unhelpful: '*trauma*' just
means a wound in Greek; nothing more complex than that.
And, no, it wasn't an awful experience at the time at all. I
was very innocent and sheltered. Bad things had been going
on in the city, of course, but I think the facts had been
carefully kept from me. *I* thought I was going on a holiday
to some auntie and uncle in England. I'd never met them,
but I had masses of aunts and uncles and we used to post
around in the summer holidays staying with them in places
like Salzburg and Bad Ischel. It all seemed fairly normal to
me. My parents saw me off at the Westbahnhof. It was a
fine day, I remember, and I was just surprised because I was
made to take my winter coat with me. I was a bit sorry too
that my sister wasn't coming, but she was fourteen and it
seemed natural that she wouldn't necessarily go on the same
trip as me. There were lots of other kids and it was very
jolly. A bigger boy called Heinrich Steiner, whom I knew
because his father was our doctor, had been told to look
after me, and I was flattered and pleased that he paid attention
to me. In the train, the two people in charge of us got us to
sing and play guessing games to pass the time. I remember
it as a happy journey, I tell you.'

'And when exactly – ?'

'June 1939.'

'No, actually I mean, when did you realize . . . ?'

'That I wasn't coming home again? Oh . . . Not for
months, not really. I told you, I was an innocent middle-
class child from a culture where children were coddled and
encouraged to conform. And when it did begin to dawn on
me that this visit was going on rather a long time, by then
I'd learnt some English and got attached to the couple who
were fostering me. I was lucky: they were nice. Really kind,
good people. They weren't young then, they've been dead
now for years. They both died well before I was married –
you never met them, did you? A lot of refugee kids didn't
fare so well. And anyway, they didn't say to me, "You're

never going home again". Well, of course they didn't. They just said, "Now the war's started you'll have to stay on a bit, Joe. You'll be able to go back home again when it's over." '

'So it was years before you really knew . . . ?'

'Yes of course. It was years before anyone *really knew* what had been going on, you may recall. *Nacht und Nebel* . . . By 1944 I was twelve – thirteen. An English grammar school boy. German gone all rusty.'

When *did* I really know? I'm not sure I've ever really known? 'Never again.' Yes. But 'never' is a word that falls to bits when you try to hold it. You can't experience 'never' at any one moment. Just as well.

'But', Mary persisted, 'it must have been dreadful for your mother and father seeing you off like that. You must have picked something up. I mean, even if they put a brave face on it for you, *they* must have known they might never see you again – or had a horrid suspicion about it, anyway.'

'I'm not at all sure about that, even.'

'Oh surely . . . I mean, it was fear of what might lie ahead that made them send you away from them, wasn't it? The ultimate parental sacrifice.'

'Yes, that seems logical to you, doesn't it?' he said flatly, obscurely angered by her articulateness. 'But what you don't realize is, many people don't function like that. There's a lot of doublethink that goes on. Not seeing things quite clearly because it's just too terrifying to do so. Oh, of course my parents were afraid – afraid for me, afraid for themselves – but they could have got out themselves, actually. I discovered that long after I was grown up. Right up to outbreak of war and even after . . . Some semi-relations in America were prepared to sponsor them. But it would have meant leaving everything and going in the clothes they stood up in. They didn't think they could do that. They were quite comfortably off. To leave my father's business, their savings, the apartment, the furniture – it went right against the faith they had lived by. I think, in the end, they were lost really because they couldn't abandon their bloody furniture.'

'Tell me more,' said Mary.

But he suddenly felt that, in spite of her sympathy and whether she herself knew it or not, she was stashing away what he told her as material for her next-but-one children's book. He said:

'No. Not now. I tell you, Mary; it's all so distant.'

After a few moments brooding, she continued pertinaciously:

'But if your journey from Austria to England seemed a happy one at the time, doesn't that just make the point? You were lulled into believing you were safe. But afterwards, and in retrospect, you came to realize what the journey had been for you. The ending of a whole way of life – a sort of death, even for you. Naturally all journeys now disturb you: you don't want to be caught out again.'

'Very neat,' he said sourly.

'And this time you're going back to Austria even. Just the same trip, in mirror image. No wonder you feel bad.'

'Yes, yes,' he told her, 'I do get the point, you needn't elaborate so.' (She always did, that was one of her maddening as well as endearing characteristics.) 'And, as it happens – but perhaps you didn't know this? – I'm not flying back with the rest of you but going on to Vienna afterwards for four days on a work trip, so that makes your mirror-image theory even neater, doesn't it? But I really don't buy it, Mary. Oh, the general journey thing perhaps, but not this bit of it. Because I've been back to Vienna – well, literally half a dozen times I should think over the years, one way and another. So the neurotic trap you seem to be indicating for me should surely be sprung by now?'

There was a pause, then she said:

'But isn't the point about neurosis that it's a trap that *can't* be sprung so easily? It can't go out of date because it's out of date already. Didn't someone say that a neurosis is like a memorial plaque to an obsolete situation? Something like that, anyway.'

'Yes. Freud did, as it happens. Among a great many other things, not all of them generally true or useful. Freud knew only his own Viennese Jewish bourgeois world and refused to believe that the conclusions he drew from it might not have universal validity. That blinkered vision's a neurosis too, as a matter of fact.'

– See, Mary, I can beat you at this tiresome game.

'Psychiatry is bunk, then?' she said slyly after a moment.

'Yes, if you like. "Cutting the Viennese hobgoblin down to size", I think Nabokov called it. And he knew what he was talking about; he had to leave his country of origin too.'

'So did Freud, I seem to remember. Fifteen-all.'

'Not till he was about eighty and had no ideas left. Thirty-fifteen!'

They laughed, in mutual relief now at discarding the too-serious for a joke. Thus released, Joe felt able to say:

'Actually Freud himself devised the perfect "Heads I win, tails you lose" situation; that's one of the many things I've got against Freudianism. If you agree with him, then you agree with him. And if not that just proves you're erecting "defences" against him, so it's game to him anyway. A sneaky way of beating patients down, I think you will agree.'

Mary laughed again and let it go at that. What she doesn't realize, he thought, deciding to abandon the half-nibbled debris of his breakfast but looking hopefully round for more coffee – what she doesn't realize, and I'm not going to tell her, is that Freud had another trick up his sleeve. He created the situation whereby for someone of my origins, my background, to be against him is a form of sacrilege. To deny Freud on the way to Freud's own city, which begot him and made his work possible, is like denying God in the temples.

Freud's city. Wittgenstein's city. Also Viktor Adler's and Schoenberg's and Mahler's and Schnzitler's and Stefan Zweig's and Klimt's and Kokoschka's and Egon Schiele's. And Theodore Herzl's. Also Karl Lueger's – Lueger who 'decided who was a Jew'. Also, for a significant while, Adolf Hitler's city. Also Eichmann's. 'The streets of Vienna are paved with culture,' said Karl Kraus, when it was still the city of liberated Jews, that famous all-pervasive cosmopolitan intelligentsia. And yet a city that was fundamentally

Catholic, provincial, philistine, nationalistic – anti-Semitic. The city where Freud exalted the importance of the individual to the status of a cult was also the place where Hitler, in his years of house-painting obscurity, incubated the ideas that were to destroy the individual, in millions, almost without a protest. And Karl Kraus, the all-seeing, produced as his only comment, 'About Hitler, nothing occurs to me to say.' What price then, the famous way that men from different professions all knew each other, all frequented the same coffee houses and sat side by side in the same auditoriums? The contractions of comic opera made real: Mahler going to consult Freud, on his way passing Zweig on the corner of Kartnerstrasse while Schnzitler was looking out of a window opposite . . . Bring on the Gipsy band. City of Dreams, it has been called. *Wien, Stadt meine Traüme* – not trauma. And this Vienna is my city of dreams, the one I like to think was my natural inheritance, the one where my true cultural roots lie and where I would have taken my proper place, had the patterns of European fate gone differently.

But in reality it *is* only a dream city in my mind, because I left it when I was so young, because I have known it since only as a visitor or at second hand. Through books and through the nostalgic memories of heavy, ageing men with accented English and un-English, oddly feminine hand-movements; those who are my father figures in default of any other . . . And because, in any case, that Vienna was dying in the 1930s, even when I was born. And even before that, in 1918, when it lost its Empire, its rôle and its wealth, emerging from the war a spiritually mutilated place, a wounded city in fact – and *Traüme* after all but trauma. Not a city of dreams but of doom. Central Europeans, you will have noticed, enjoy such meaningful puns, which most English people think are tiresome.

Who am I? The exile's insistent, self-pitying cry.

I am Joe Beech, a good English-sounding name, joint director of a prosperous publishing firm I helped to found in easier times than these, with a degree from Oxford, married to a Protestant English woman for nearly twenty-five years (can it be?) and father of two agnostic English children.

I am also, or was, Josef Buchsbaum. In Vienna that is a good Jewish name, and indeed my grandparents on both sides emerged from the traditional world of Galician Jewry. My parents' generation, of course, was 'assimilated'; Viennese first, as they thought, their Jewishness reduced to a small mystery, just something *there*. Buchsbaum is the German for 'beech tree', but when I was a very small boy, learning avidly to read, it pleased me that *Buch* (different sound but the same letters) was also a book. Happy little prig that I no doubt was, son of ambitious parents, I liked the idea of myself as a book-tree. So was I the publisher-designate already?

My father, in the import-export business, was the one who represented plain worldly ambition: my mother, I believe, went in more for culture. (I think that is almost, if not quite, how they themselves would have expressed it; though it must be said that if you lose your parents in childhood you spend the rest of your life helplessly attempting to edit memory for an adult version of them.) My mother was also, I surmise, the one with the more romantic temperament. She had in her room a volume of pictures I now know to be by Klimt which I liked to look through, charmed if slightly amazed by the hair and the gold, by the all-consuming sexuality my infant mind half-perceived there. My sister had abundant curling hair too. My mother let me look through the book but told me not to mention to my father that I had done so. (I have often pondered that memory inconclusively, wondering what it may tell me about her, my father, myself.) But she also had a public Klimt reproduction, so to speak, on the wall over her toilet table. It was his 'Beechwoods', an anodyne harmony of reds and purples brindled with light. I appreciated it as an object (and recognized another print of it years later with a shock of delight) but I am fairly sure I also thought, with a small child's egocentricity, that because of our name the picture had a personal link with me.

It did, as matters turned out. But we did not know it. But what, earlier, was there to 'know'? The perpetual conundrum.

The German for beechwoods is *Buchenwald*. Such terrible meaning Klimt's innocent picture has posthumously been given: such transformations.

> *Simple goodbyes to children or friends become*
> *A felon's numb*
> *Farewell, and love that was warm, a meeting place –*
> *Love is the suicide's grave under the nettles.*

The announcement system crackled. The plane was preparing to land at Vienna. (No, of course, how stupid of him: it was not Vienna but Zurich. Vienna still lay a whole week away, and infinitely more distant in terms of the circuitous endeavour that must be undergone before reaching it.)

He suddenly saw the week's skiing as if it were a landscape laid out on end, one vast and enormously difficult terrain to be traversed, an immense snowy waste of heights and depths, aching climbs and dangerous precipices. Rocks, a far-off frozen lake, the silent abysses beneath the fragile, clanking lifts . . . Would he really have the mental and physical stamina to cross it? Would he and his small tribe have the luck to cross it all without mishap? Now, in immediate prospect, the labour of trying to ensure everyone else's safety, let alone his own, in this treacherous ice-world terrified him.

When the children were young – when he himself had been relatively younger – he had never worried particularly about their safety. Now in secret (Caroline must not know, it would only make *her* worse) he found himself worrying almost obsessionally.

He told himself that this was irrational and anyway useless: the children were grown, they were not stupid. They had been taught the right skills and given the appropriate warnings; to agonize so about their safety was as pointless as

26

agonizing about the safety of contemporaries – which, as a matter of fact, he also did these days. But it did not feel pointless or irrational to him. On the contrary, he felt obscurely that he worried now because the time had come to do so. And it wasn't even that well-known trick: 'If I worry about it then it won't actually happen.' It was rather: 'I'd better worry about it, I've got to think about it – to try to get on to terms with it. To be prepared, just a bit, in advance.'

Prepared for what, for God's sake?

For this – this awful Thing that is going to happen. Is – perhaps – may – will . . . Anyway: this Thing.

As the plane landed with the smallest of bumps, he was already travelling rapidly in his mind across vast snowscapes, probing the contours obsessionally and inconclusively, seeking the hidden abyss.

2

In the coach that was to take them from Zurich across the border, into Austria and the mountains, Joe found himself next to Lisette.

'Abandoned David then?' he said with forced paternal jocularity. She said in a lowered tone, rather shyly as if confessing a weakness:

'I thought it would be nice for Jerome if David sat with him for a bit. As Jerome was on his own on the plane.'

Had Caroline been coaching her? But, looking into Lisette's dark-fringed eyes with their clear whites, and receiving a nervous, almost placatory smile in response, Joe did not think so. He said gently, 'That was very thoughtful of you, Lisette.'

She sat beside him, solid and pretty with her dark curling hair and her pink-and-blue snowsuit, and he thought that he hardly knew her, this girl whom David had, with apparent brusque casualness, introduced into their lives half way through the past year. Attempting to take his cue from his son, he had at first regarded her as transient, just one of a procession of attractive but not-always-readily-distinguishable faces of both sexes that came and went in his house, ate his food (usually with polite thanks) and monopolized his telephone. It had been well into the autumn before it had dawned on him one Sunday, when David had come down from York for the weekend (it had been Caroline's birthday) that his son loved this particular girl. David had, with unaccustomed tentativeness, as if he feared a rebuff, brought up the idea that Lisette might be invited to join the proposed skiing party, and when Joe and Caroline, dutifully, parentally amiable, said 'Yes, by all means' David had telephoned back to York that very afternoon. Passing the open study door, Joe had caught the tone of his voice rather than the words. Its private yearning gentleness had caused an unexpected pang in his own heart.

Since then, Lisette had been seen in their house a number of times, though in public David treated her in much the same offhand way he treated one of his sister's friends. Joe had registered that she had nice manners and that Caroline (thank heavens) approved of her. She appeared to come from a cultured family, indeed she had overcome David's longterm, schoolboy resistance to classical music: the sounds that emanated from David's room these days were no longer the unremitting heavy beat that had signalled his presence since his early teens. But only now, as she turned her face towards him in the bus, did Joe see belatedly – how could he have missed it before? – that Lisette was beautiful.

He said after a minute: 'It's nice of you to think of Jerome; I won't discourage you. I know his mother's a little afraid he might end up the odd one out. Particularly as he's not a very good skier. David's rather good, in a lumbering sort of way – or was last time I saw him – and I gather you've skied quite a bit?'

'Oh I'm not really *good*,' she said at once. 'But I did learn when I was little and that helps. I do love it; it's such fun.'

'Oh God,' said Joe suddenly, cutting her short.

'What is it?' She looked scared. 'Have you lost something?' The bus engine was starting up.

'Yes – No – But I must – Excuse me a moment!' He struggled out of the seat, over her legs, and ran down the aisle.

'Please!' he said desperately to the driver in German. 'I have made a mistake: I need something from the bag that I let you put in the luggage compartment. A medicament,' he added untruthfully.

Inured to the early morning behaviour of skiing parties, the man pulled on the brake he had just released, pressed the button to open the door again, and allowed Joe to accompany him down onto the pavement again. The bag in question took a while to extract: the man stood by resignedly while Joe repossessed it, with copious apologies, and they both regained the bus.

'What on earth – ?' said Caroline, craning forward as Joe

29

marched up the aisle, bag in his arms. He gave her a wide, inane grin and took refuge further up in his seat beside Lisette. The bag was too big for the overhead rack, which is why he had thoughtlessly relinquished it in the first place. He prepared to hug it to him for the three-hour journey.

'Something important?' said Lisette respectfully.

'Just a notebook.'

'Oh. I thought it might be some work you wanted to do on this ride. Daddy does that sometimes, and Mum and I wonder how he *can* – in a coach or a car, I mean. We would get sick.'

'Yes, so would I. I can't work on a bus. It's just – well, this notebook is rather important to me, and I suddenly panicked about having let it out of my hands. Stupid, really, I know.' And indeed, in Lisette's consoling company, it did suddenly seem stupid. What possible harm did he imagine could have come to it in the luggage hold? Yet he had had a clear, sickening image of the bag in which it was stowed simply not being in the hold when they reached their destination: carelessly off-loaded at some earlier stop, left forlorn on a snowy roadside or carried off into an unknown house by some uncaring stranger. His Notebook. Absurd in any case, probably, to set such store by a notebook, as if it really held, or ever would hold, the key to anything. But his reaction at the thought of its disappearance had been instinctive, overwhelming.

Attempting to regain his composure and forestall any further question about the notebook from Lisette – not that she seemed about to ask any – he asked her:

'What does your father do? I don't think David's ever mentioned that to me.'

'Daddy? He's an accountant.' She looked wistful. 'He works terribly hard, much harder than he need. Mum and I are always trying to think up tricks to get him to take a bit more time off. Dan used to as well – he's my brother – but now Dan's getting as bad as Daddy himself. And the trouble is, *he* knows Mum's and my tricks to get people to stop

working so he sees through them much more than Daddy
does; we're having to invent new ones!'

Joe had a sudden, complete mental picture, as through the
wrong end of an opera glass, of this family: the ambitious,
uneven-tempered father, the clever young son taking after
him; the women ganging up on them in an age-old pattern,
adoring but censorious. Was Lisette's mother beautiful too?
A shared female complicity and confidence, rivalry
unnecessary.

His own children, reared in another, less close and
coherent pattern, would not, he thought, create such an
instant image of their family life for others. In any case he
doubted whether they chattered so readily about their home
life at all. Humbly he said:

'It's kind of your parents to spare you to us for this week.
I hope they don't mind you going off again when you've
only recently come home?'

'Oh *no*. I mean . . .' she hesitated and looked sideways at
Joe: 'Well, actually I think Daddy was just a bit sad when I
left but he didn't think he ought to be, if you know what I
mean. And Mum was pleased for me: she doesn't ski herself
but she's always liked us to ski. And she really likes David.'

'Oh – good,' said Joe inadequately, trying to imagine his
son impressing these unknown people.

'They said,' Lisette continued, evidently seizing her opportunity to deliver a message with which she had been
entrusted: 'That it would be very nice if you and Caroline
and David could come up to us one Sunday for lunch. We're
not very far off the M1. Perhaps next holidays, if there isn't
time these. Jennifer too, of course, if she can.'

'Well, that would be very nice,' he said, at sea in the
intricacies of these new, potential relationships, mind spiral-
ling into the hypothetical future. 'Will you say so to your
parents from us, and thank them?'

She nodded, pleased. After a moment she said:

'It's a shame Jennifer couldn't have come on this trip, isn't
it?'

She means it, he thought. She isn't just being diplomatic,

31

she's too young. She just thinks it's a pity I can't have my own loved daughter with me, and she's right. She has all the right instincts. Loved child – lovely, complete female creature: daughter of a united family. Not spoiled. *Brought up in love and fear*. No wonder David wants her for his own.

I expect he wants her family for his own too. They sound as if they have a number of advantages over Caroline and me. Mr and Mrs Mendel. Lisette Mendel. Well, well.

The bus left Zurich and its lake behind, passed through other towns and villages. By and by they crossed the Austrian frontier – waved through without ceremony as if history had never been – and began to climb. Soon patches of dirty snow appeared by the side of the road, vestiges of an early December fall and thaw; later the whole landscape began imperceptibly to whiten, with a recent powdery fall through which the bones of the earth still showed. The sky, brilliant at dawn, was now at the end of the morning opaque and uncertain. On the bus, a state of suspended watchfulness prevailed; people spoke respectfully of snow reports, of temperatures, of recent or projected blizzards. Presently they stopped at a large roadside café, and most of the passengers went busily in search of sandwiches, beer or lavatories. Unattracted by these options, Joe got down and lingered in the open air, stamping his feet, sniffing hopefully for a chill whiff of the mountains which he could now see clearly but not yet feel.

All journeys to a ski resort were basically the same journey: the departure in the night, the aching hours of travel, the abrupt concentration on one idea. He had not been in Heiligenhof before, but he knew already what it would be like: the houses with ornately carved balconies, the one main street crowded with people in brightly coloured clothes moving with that ungainly rolling gait peculiar to humans walking in modern ski boots, the busy coffee shops and bars. A carnival place, a stage-set: *Der Zigeunerbaron* in winter guise; a mock-medieval scene, skis carried shoulder high like jousting lances; *Gemütlichkeit* personified, the taste of *Glühwein* on the tongue; a sweet claustrophobia to defy the mountains hanging all around, great, intimidating, unpopulated spaces.

And just as all ski villages were one, so in memory were all skiing holidays one, as if time stopped again and again in the same place. As the bus continued on its way, climbing more steeply now, its passengers variously refreshed and relieved and chattering more, Joe became aware in himself of an absurd sense of elation as if they really were travelling into the known happiness and safety of the past – as if, in this village that was all the villages, he would find a younger David and Jerome, bombing down the nursery slopes, legs spread, a young Jennifer clutching at his hand as the T-bar lift jerked them upwards; a younger Tom and Mary and Caroline and other friends besides: known jokes, known paths, known and long-consumed meals, everything the same, the same, without surcease, not hell but a small heaven going on for ever . . . *Heiligenhof.* The hallowed house.

His mood of euphoria lasted while they drove the final, winding miles into Heiligenhof. Here faith was rewarded: the magic had worked. The first really heavy snows of winter lay thick and flocculent, bandaging the earth, weighting the trees. Snow ploughs, they were told, had been out early that morning to keep open the road they were now travelling. Groups of passengers were deposited at two large, new hotels on the outskirts of the village, and the bus came to its final stop outside the small railway station. A bright girl with the name of the tour company straining across her yellow sateen breast told the Beeches and the Lovells to wait: she was just going to escort another group to their hotel and then she would be back to show them where their guesthouse was. It was, she assured them, beaming, the nicest and most conveniently situated chalet in the place.

Impatient already to explore, they fidgeted in the little square. The brief winter afternoon was beginning to decline; the mountain on one side was still bright with tiny, wheeling figures, visible against its whiteness, but on the opposite heights a great shadow had already fallen.

'It isn't as cold as I thought it would be,' said Lisette, sounding almost disappointed.

'Not cold enough, in my opinion,' said Tom Lovell, sniffing like a gun dog. 'A bit too damp. We're going to lose a lot of this nice snow again if the temperature doesn't drop tonight.' He gestured disparagingly at the dripping Gothic eaves and gurgling gutters, and no one could contradict him. 'Landslide weather,' he said.

As if in graphic response to the word, Joe's stomach sank. Landslide indeed. The just-possible horror that lurked at the heart of every skiing holiday: the ineradicable danger inherent in the nature of the sport. The hidden abyss. Oh, God.

'Oh, for heaven's sake, Tom!' said Mary, and then, to the assembled company: 'I'm so sorry, everyone. He can't bear not to be a Job's comforter. Tom, couldn't you find something else to entertain us with while we're waiting? A nice, encapsulated worry to get our teeth into – what about the hire shop having run out of boots? Or the chalet having no hot water?'

'If the shop's out of boots that's your funeral, not mine,' said Tom comfortably. 'I've got my own boots. So's Joe – eh, haven't you, Joe? It's you girls that'll be in trouble.'

'And the kids.'

'I just hope the shop's got boots *big* enough for me,' said Jerome mournfully.

'What size do you take?' asked Joe, eyeing this great rangy young man, whom he remembered so well as a confiding five-year-old collecting beetles and interrogating Joe on his belief in God. (It was eventually agreed between them that there probably wasn't one, but you never knew.) David was taller than his own father but Jerome was a head taller again. Of course Mary was a big-boned woman.

'Eleven,' said Jerome without pride.

'Let's see . . . That's about 46 or 47 Continental style?'

'Is it? I always forget. That's another thing: I forget from one time to another what boots are supposed to feel like – I mean, how uncomfortable they're supposed to be. I

34

remember when I first came skiing my boots were – oh, really awful, but I didn't realize. Then my toenails started bleeding. Do you remember, Mum?'

'Indeed I do,' said Mary with feeling. 'I felt such a bad mother. Letting one's child wear boots that don't fit! The classic maternal failure. Like not putting knickers on little girls, or shutting them in cupboards to stop them being afraid of the dark . . . Where is that blasted yellow person? I'm beginning to want a chalet girl to welcome me with tea and homemade cake.'

Several of Mary's books for children had nineteenth-century settings. But their underlying feeling belied, Joe had always felt, the charming Kate-Greenaway-cum-Phiz illustrations with which their publisher provided them. For Mary, apparently, the past was not a place of safety or comfort. 'Ms Lovell is not afraid to deal in subjects which, twenty years ago, would have been considered too strong meat for children's literature', a critic had written last year. 'This new, and very accomplished work, tackles almost incidentally both child-death and a cruel father. Behind the Dickensian picnics and donkey rides, fear lurks.'

The books, in fact, did not seem to come out of Mary's own Home Counties, twentieth-century childhood (as far as Joe understood it) but to have another genesis: he sensed a whiff of the *Struwwelpeter* world of his own earliest literary memories; good dog Tray beaten, Conrad with his thumbs cut off, Maria burnt to death by playing with matches. Intrigued, he had once tried to talk to Mary about her work, but she either could not or would not be drawn, behaving indeed as he did when she tried to probe the centre of him. 'I don't know where my books come from. If I did know, perhaps I wouldn't be able to write them. Don't be a *bore* Joe, it's not like you. You're being like the sort of person one meets at a party. Any minute you'll be saying "It must be wonderful to be a writer. Mind you, I could write a book if I had the time." '

Impenetrable Mary, both warm and cool. Mary, whose cluttered room in an Oxford college long ago had been a refuge for undergraduates of both sexes less assured and developed than herself; Mary, who could still be relied on to manage everyone, to turn a difficult conversation, to disperse an incipient argument with a joking display – 'my circus horse act', as she had once referred to it. Yet once – when? – about two years ago now, he had been saying to Caroline after some joint theatre party how marvellously Mary managed old Tom, who really was becoming a bit of a bore with his philistine-tycoon act, and Caroline had amazed him by hinting that she knew more, and otherwise. Mary and Tom, she intimated, had been having 'a bad time' recently; they must all hope for the best, but . . .

Initially irritated by Caroline's air of self-conscious discretion, of knowing more (for once) than he did and not being prepared to reveal all she knew, Joe had been inclined to dismiss what she said as exaggeration. Obviously the Lovells argued and always had; two such vociferous people could hardly not argue, and what was wrong with that? (Caroline herself had never understood the conventions of argument, retreating instead into a pained silence.)

But her pregnant words had remained in his mind. And by and by he had come to see that they were probably true. Mary had looked ill two years ago. White and puffy and smoking constantly. She looked better now. Let us hope for the best indeed; let us pass on hastily, trusting that Mary, of all people, will do the right thing. In his present weakness, the very idea of two of his oldest friends breaking up was more than Joe could bear. A miserably self-centred view of events, he knew, but it was the best he could do just now. If there is an abyss here I don't want to know about it. And perhaps it is now past and over anyway, and they are safe on the other side of it . . . He stood in the cold square watching his friends, suddenly possessed by a yearning envy and weariness.

Caroline too stood slightly apart. In her, as well, there was envy, but that was a more or less chronic emotion with her these days, and she was not feeling particularly tired, merely tense and anxious to get to the chalet and stop worrying about bedroom allocation and hard beds and hot water and whether there would be a lavatory near their room and how much competition there would be for that and the showers. There were never enough of either in the chalets. She would have relished a proper hotel with private bathrooms, but would have been sincerely shocked, and censorious, had Joe proposed anything so extravagant for a family holiday. It would be bad for the children, who did not need to have such luxury handed to them. The Lovells could have afforded it easily, of course, but they probably felt the same. That was the sort of thing she and Mary agreed about.

Mary may seem very full of herself now, Caroline thought, but she wasn't the spring before last. I remember the four of us going to that tiresome, smart play about adultery and her ringing me up the next day and suddenly bursting into tears on the phone. Mary, of all people. Of course I asked her to lunch.

I thought at first after that play (but of course it was just a play, not necessarily true to life at all) that she was upset because she – or Tom – or both of them . . . People can hurt each other so much, it's terrible, I won't think about that . . . But, from what she said, I understood that it was more that she felt she was having some sort of general crackup. Well, she said 'crisis' but I thought, and still think, that 'crackup' is a better word for what she was going through. She didn't seem in the least like herself. I'd say, if it wasn't such an odd, out-of-date word, that she was like someone *possessed*. But by what? Some sickness – fever – I don't know . . . She seemed *driven*. She talked of leaving Tom, of changing her whole way of life 'before it was too late' – God knows what.

Well, I talked her out of it. At least I think I must have. At any rate she didn't leave Tom, and they seem much jollier together now. And she said afterwards that talking to me that day had helped. I was so pleased when she said that. I know I'm not clever or original like her, I don't amuse people – let alone being frightfully clever and beautiful with it like Anna Morley: I used to be so jealous of them both when I first got married, oh God it hurt so: Joe's old friends: I knew they weren't that impressed by me, though they tried to be kind . . . But at least I've got a certain amount of common sense. I couldn't have brought up the children and taught part-time and looked after Joe and been a JP if I hadn't got sense. I tell myself that.

But recently – well, for a couple of years actually – I haven't felt right somehow. Not right somewhere down inside myself. And it's worse now that David's away at university and Jenn's got her own flat. Both of them gone. I miss them so, more than I ever thought I would. I tell myself I always knew they would leave home one day – that's the point of it all, that children should grow up and go away. I left home myself when I was even younger than Jenn – but telling myself doesn't make it any better. Their empty, tidy rooms . . .

I don't go on about it. What's the use? It only makes things worse. I know Joe minds a lot too: he goes into great bad-tempered glooms when David goes back to York, when Jenn . . . Either that or he's out a lot. He's so selfish. He behaves as if he's the only person who suffers.

If only I didn't have this wretched cystitis. It's been going on – oh, for several years now, sometimes almost gone and then insidiously worse again: this sickening soreness, this distracting feeling you want to Go when you don't really . . . It's worse again this afternoon: the strain of the journey, probably. The doctor says it would trouble me less if I could learn to relax more: what fatuous advice, you *can't* relax when you've got it, that's the point about it.

Sometimes I think that the cystitis is probably the cause of my bad feeling – that I'd feel much better about life in general if I didn't have it. But at other times I wonder if it's the other way round – I mean, if it's something wrong in my life that's giving me cystitis. What? I don't know . . .

If it stays bad like this all the week, how will I ever manage skiing? It was bad last winter too, but we didn't go skiing then; Joe went to that publishers' conference or whatever it was, in New York, and couldn't take more time off. The winter before? I think it wasn't so bad just then. Managing skiing of all things: having to keep up with a group and go where they go, nervous tension, the awful loos they have in mountain cafés and not many of them, all those straps and zips to undo . . . Oh God, how will I cope, why am I here?

I wish Jennifer was here too. We've never really talked about it, but I know she understands how I feel – what it's like to be pushed into doing something you don't really want to because Joe and David enjoy it and you have to pretend you're enjoying it too or everyone thinks you're a wet blanket and resents you. Jenn tried awfully hard at skiing a few years ago, she really did, but it isn't basically her sort of thing any more than it is mine – so exhausting and uncomfortable and frightening. If she were here she would be a sort of unspoken support to me, but of course it's because she doesn't really like it either that she isn't here.

If she were here then she and Lisette could share the other room and there wouldn't be all this jokey, underhand stuff going on about who sleeps where. It isn't right, Lisette's only eighteen. She seems nicely brought up, so what would her family think about it? I don't care *what's* 'usual at university' these days – all this sharing – mixed flats and so on – can't parents still be responsible, still set an example? Joe identifies too much with David, and he's too soft. I know Lisette's a nice little thing – a pretty little Jewish girl – but that's really not a reason for Joe to gaze at her in that fatuously admiring way I saw him doing in the bus. Nor is it a reason for him tacitly to encourage her and David into bed with each other. Their relationship won't necessarily last. They're too young. And when he says to me in that maddening, expansive, over-tolerant way, 'Well, we were almost as young as them . . .', that's missing the point. *We* were too young – or I was . . .

I read somewhere once, in a novel, that sex is like a journey. I didn't think much of that at the time – I mean, novelists do make such an extravagant fuss about these things – but the idea stayed in my mind and I've thought about it sometimes since. I suppose that, if it's a journey, then if you start out on the right route you eventually come, perhaps via a few false turnings, maybe years later, to where you are meant to be, yes, you come, I am told you come . . . But if you start out on the wrong route then you end up down a blocked alley. I find myself imagining it being like some dreary housing estate where the roads lead nowhere. Or, worse, no roads at all: just a ditch and hedge and brambles. Stupid pictures, but they just come into my mind, bad-dream places.

When you have cystitis, sex hurts. Or even if it doesn't hurt that particular night you think it's going to so you tense up: you lose your nerve about it. And sex itself makes cystitis worse, that's well known: nuns never get it. So doing it at all becomes an heroic act; you feel you've achieved something just in letting your husband in there, knowing all the while that it'll do no good. In such circumstances, any question of what I believe is called 'satisfaction' becomes largely irrelevant. Of course it does.

Sometimes in book shops – after all, I am a woman of my own time, not really the repressed Victorian all this makes me feel – I look surreptitiously into books about what fun sex is, and all the things you can do . . . I might as well be reading travel books about Thailand or Outer Mongolia: it couldn't be more alien.

Oh, perhaps people are just making a lot of it up. Sex *can't* be as important as that, it just can't, or people like me would never survive as well as we do. And just think of all the people who have lived, and do live, without sex at all, and been great thinkers or creators or visionaries. That is reality, that is permanence, not all this obsessive fiddling round with bodies. Small minded. Dirty minded . . . I won't even think about this any more. Sex isn't necessarily more real than anything else, it's just people like Joe who think so. Life can be lived on other levels. Thank goodness.

Oh, I do hope the cats will be all right. I did warn Mrs B. about that irritation Zilla gets on her ears sometimes, but she hasn't got her eye in for the signs of it like I have, like

Jenn has. And the rabbits! Oh no, I mustn't think about the rabbits, I'm not really entirely happy about the Turner boys having them, but what could I do, so soon after Christmas? I just hope they clean the poor dears out often enough. I kept telling David he *must* explain to Simon Turner how important that is, and of course all I got was 'Oh Mu-um, don't fuss'. It's so unfair, they're David's rabbits – or were years ago, when he was still at school – and now he's away all the time and doesn't do a damn thing about them, I have to make all the arrangements and slog round finding greens for them. I just hope the Turner boys realize how much they need. Soft, vulnerable, baby things, helpless in their hutches, baby-buntings in rabbit skins. Oh how can anyone kill and eat rabbits, that used to make me so miserable as a child. When I think about them something softens – moves – flows inside me, almost like thinking about a baby you are breast-feeding . . . Long ago. Life worked then.

Oh thank goodness, there's that girl in yellow coming back at last, we're all getting frozen here. I do so need a cup of tea. And a loo.

At supper in the chalet dining room the seven members of the Lovell-Beech party occupied one end of the long table in an integrated block. (Chalets, in the words of the company's brochure, 'encourage a family-style atmosphere rather than the formal separate tables of the costlier hotel accommodation.') The eight other, strange members of this week's instant 'family' were more fragmentarily grouped down the rest of the table: two hopeful-looking secretaries who glanced, between mouthfuls of boeuf bourguignon at David and Jerome, a middle-aged Scottish couple who could be heard speaking firmly of the joys of the new skiing centre at Aviemore in tones that suggested a faint disparagement of Switzerland, France and indeed Austria, and two unremarkable men with a plump woman who seemed to be accompanying both of them. There was also an extra, youngish man, thin and fevered with a Birmingham accent and without a companion, but who had already made it clear before supper that he was 'really with the fellows next door' and that it was oversight or over-booking on the part of the chalet company that had landed him in this house. He, Joe gathered, was to be Jerome's roommate. Joe, humping cases to the top floor, had missed the moment of decision, but evidently David and Lisette were going to share one room. It seemed to have been accomplished rapidly without discussion, and, amused, he suspected Mary's hand in the matter. Caroline – had she yet realized? – would not be pleased.

Joe promised himself that tomorrow night he would make more effort about the disparate Others – that he would encourage his own tribe, who had such an advantage of collective numbers, to abandon their comfortable, exclusive closeness and make the Others feel less out of things. Particularly that agonizing boy, and those two girls who were presumably already hoping that Lisette was not a girlfriend but a little sister, and who would, alas, be unlikely to appeal to Jerome: one he mentally christened the White Mouse and the other Miss Piggy.

But tonight was the time for his own tribe's exclusiveness, the moment, after the tensions of the journey, to re-knit the old ties, without need yet to take up new positions. A time for almost-sentimental reminiscences of past seasons and innocent high hopes, as yet untainted by failures, disappointments or frustrations, of the pristine week to come. Do you remember? 'Do you remember when David and Jerome were thirteen or fourteen and Joe and Tom *would* let them come on that black run above Courcheval – yes you *did*, Tom, it was your fault just as much as Joe's – and Jerome got stuck and had to be talked down?' . . . 'Do you remember, for that matter, when *Mary* lost her nerve on that glacier?' . . . 'Do you remember that fantastic day on the Italian holiday?' . . . 'Do you remember the adulterous pig-farmer at Zöll who would ask us every day at breakfast where we were going and then turn up there too?' – 'He was dead bored, poor man, by his accomplice in sin.' – 'Serve him right, it's a known hazard!' . . . 'Do you remember that awful time years and years ago when we'd gone somewhere too late in the season, or not high enough or something' – 'St Cernin?' – 'Yes, that's right, and there was that terrifying sleet and we kept getting wet right through to our knickers.' . . . 'We didn't know so much then.' – 'Speak for yourself; I've forgotten most of what I knew then.' 'That was before the children came.' 'That was before they were *invented*.' – 'That's what I mean. Even Jerome wasn't thought of then' . . . 'Wasn't that St Cernin holiday the one soon after you and Joe got married, Caroline?' Caroline agreed that was so.

The children, abruptly de-invented by the vertiginous backwards-passage of memory, listened now in indulgent silence as their parents, contracted to a long-ago foursome, babbled on.

Now Tom was holding forth on Joe and Caroline's wedding, his face glowing in one of his intermittent fits of sentiment that sat oddly these days on his more customary manner of abrasive cynicism.

' . . . One of those frightfully cold winters,' he was saying nostalgically, 'in the days before anyone had proper central heating, and cars would be pigs to start and you had to do it on the handle. I remember cranking and cranking that old Morris of mine, thinking she'd never turn over, with Joe and Mary going spare inside and yelling contradictory advice. Joe and me in hired morning suits with our balls freezing off and knowing that all the time Caro' was waiting for us at the church, eh my love? – no doubt thinking Joe really had abandoned her. All in white – sort of fluffy-looking dress somehow, silvery, like an ice-princess – and your face was dead white too by the time we did turn up!' He gave a shout of laughter, and raised his wine glass to Caroline, who looked confused but pleased.

But I could do without this particular saga, thought Joe. Tonight, and any night for that matter, but particularly tonight. Because our happiness tonight is fragile and inno-cent and uncomplicated and for that very reason should not be expected to bear too much weight. Oh, I know Tom's a bit drunk and means well, but we none of us need reminding now of the origins of matrimony. It's all too long ago: it doesn't have any relevance any more, to any of us. Too much has happened in between. If we are all still together, now, then that fact isn't, God knows, anything to do with a public ceremony twenty-five years ago that, young and crude as we were, we made too much of and yet in our deepest hearts did not take seriously enough. 'For ever.' What did we understand of 'for ever' in our twenties? What of 'as long as ye both shall live'? I, at any rate, had not known anyone live to a great age. Why, even now, I am older, already, then almost anyone I knew well then.

Tom seems simply happy to recall the bright past. So, looking at her, does Caroline. Even Mary seems quite complacent. So why am I finding this conversation painful – dangerous – ? After all, it is a fact: we *are* still – both pairs of us – together.

> . . . *If it must be so, let's nor weep nor complain;*
> *If I have failed, or you, or life turned sullen,*
> *We have had these things, they do not come again,*
> *But the flag still flies and the city has not fallen . . .*

At his elbow Lisette, who had been listening attentively to an account that was new, at least, to her, said to him softly:

'Your wedding does sound as if it was lovely in the end, even if it nearly went wrong at first.'

'To be honest, I don't remember it all that well.' And that is, actually, the truth he thought, but, realizing that it would sound ungracious, he amended:

'I expect I'd drunk rather too much. I seem to recall Tom and Mary and me having brandy in the morning, to warm ourselves up before we tried to start the car, and then all that champagne afterwards . . . I was nervous, I suppose. Terrified, in a way. Caroline seemed to have such a lot of family, and some of them rather grand in my terms. Large houses in the country and so forth. I thought they wouldn't approve of me – though of course I pretended I didn't care.'

No, I didn't exactly fear they would think me 'a common little man' though such phrases were part of the natural intimate vocabulary of Carline's mother: after all, I did have my Oxford degree to protect me, and a social veneer acquired there and as a National Service officer in a rather smart regiment living beyond my means. But I guessed they would think – know – that in spite of this good camouflage and Tom's authentic Hooray Henry backup, I was really a rootless person, landless and essentially homeless, a frequenter of cities . . . Typical Jew.

I won't say that to Lisette. Come to that, I'm not sure why I've told her that about having been terrified. Perhaps it was because she's really an outsider herself with us, wanting very much to be one of us?

No, on reflection, I believe it was because she sounded as if *she* wanted to console *me* for something.

'Did you not have as many relations there as your wife – as – as Caroline?' she asked shyly, and he answered:

'No. None. No real ones, that is. My family came from central Europe, you see.' He braced himself, as usual, to enlarge on that fact when the next question came. He had become so used to this, over the years, that he no longer found it painful, merely tiresome, to have to explain. Lisette was so young of course, born long after the war was over, he couldn't expect her . . . But it always irked him a little that many people of his own generation, who might have been expected to know better, were so obtuse, not picking up cues, having to have everything laid on the line for them. Such Anglo-Saxon insularity, when, after all, his immediate background of loss was merely the classic one for people of his kind and generation – classic to the point of banality. A trauma? *Ja, ja, ein Träuma* – so what? Horror itself made tedious and pedestrian by over-reproduction, utterly commonplace. And this devaluing providing the final touch of horror . . .

But Lisette said simply: 'So you didn't have anyone of your own to come to your wedding?'

'Friends – I had friends.'

'Oh yes, I'm *sure* you did. But – no one else at all? No one left?'

'No. All gone.' He saw he did not need to elaborate further. She bit her lip and looked at the tablecloth.

Ah, don't cry, dear Lisette, for people who were nothing and nowhere twenty years and more before you were born, people who – perhaps – (I have tried saying this to myself, attempting through words to reach some understanding of facts) – fuelled the ovens at Auschwitz or were, briefly, a pall of smoke above Majdanek or Treblinka. Or Bergen Belsen. Or maybe Buchenwald. Because I shall never know, the exact *where* and *when* (I tell myself also) make no difference. Besides my parents, my sister and two grandparents I had, I think, seven uncles and aunts, five of them with spouses, at least ten first cousins and a much larger number of more distant cousins and the like. Gone, all gone, all that sentient, well-fed, well-maintained flesh, all those minds and hearts and hopes and plans, guilts, dreams and futures. Pasts too, for all those stored individual memories went as well. Just gone. In the end, after every conceivable gesture and attitude, that's all you can say. We tend to speak and write now as if the camps were an elaborate metaphor for archetypal human evil: in fact they were built to kill the Jews. Just that.

I could never have told Caroline's family about all those people. They must have known – or guessed. Caroline knows of course, and minds for me in a shrinking way. I'm sure she's never discussed it with her family. They're the sort of English people who feel it is tasteless to refer to such unpleasant things, or even to think about them, who like to believe that reports of atrocities, or even natural disasters, are 'much exaggerated'. Caroline told me once that when she was very small, during the war, and was frightened by hearing people on a country bus talk of bombs, her mother briskly said that of course *children* did not get killed in wars. And that's called a 'good, secure upbringing'.

But it dawned on me, only a year or so ago, after Caroline's father died, that the fact that they were – are – like that was probably one of the reasons I married Caroline anyway. If one can ever talk about 'reasons'.

I was lonely, I think. My life was going well, on the surface, but I wanted to belong somewhere. Girls fell in love with me, but I wanted something more, or different. It seems improbable now, but I believe I wanted to attach myself to that whole way of life that Caroline and her kind represented: all those people living in Shropshire and Dorset and sending their sons to schools like Stowe and Wellington and Marlborough, and being country solicitors and magistrates, GPs and land owners – full of knowledge about this and that and also knowing nothing, nothing . . . That fact that they knew nothing about people like me and my background was just an added benefit. That being so, I could insinuate myself among them incognito. Oh, I didn't think of it like that at the time, but I do believe now that was how it was. And no doubt that too was why, for my best man, I asked Tom, whom they would think so suitable in every way, rather than one or two other friends who were really closer to me.

He heard Tom trumpeting now, at the head of the table. The conversation had shifted from weddings to food, and Tom was arguing with Jerome about vegetarianism. Jerome was working his father up by maintaining that, while he did not in practice care enough about the subject one way or another to be vegetarian himself, he entirely sympathized with the logic of those who were.

'Oh so do I, Jerome,' said Caroline anxiously, pushing the remains of her beef aside as if in sudden confirmation. 'I think about slaughter houses, and often I do wonder if I oughtn't really to give meat up entirely. It's not as if I'd miss it . . .'

'Slaughter houses?' said Jerome wildly, as if he'd barely heard the term before. 'I wasn't meaning that. Isn't the usual argument about the use of resources and how it's uneconomic to process vegetable matter into beef before we eat it?'

'Yes of course,' Caroline agreed. 'And we none of us *need*

meat. In fact we all eat more of most things than we really need.'

'Speak for yourself, Mum,' interrupted David rudely. 'Or rather don't, because it's not true. You're all thin and bony and should eat more anyway, and as for me I *certainly* need meat, so don't go getting any fancy ideas about converting me to lentils and things or I won't ever come home again. I know you and your puritanical ideas . . . Vegetarianism – yuk! There was this girl living in my hall on campus last year – Lisette knows her too – and she was vegetarian and kept shoving it down everyone's throat, and going on and on at us in the most boring, priggish way till we felt guilty every time we ate so much as a sausage in front of her.'

'She had pamphlets she used to give out about slaughter houses,' Lisette remarked. 'I must admit, I didn't like them.'

'She was so *wet* . . . and she thought she was so wonderful. She went to *church* too.'

'What could be more despicable!' said Mary, highly diverted.

'Were they pamphlets about Jewish and Moslem slaughter houses?' Joe asked Lisette suddenly.

'Yes – actually.' She looked unhappy.

'I thought so, I've seen them too. Covert racialism and anti-Semitism disguised as humanitarianism.' He saw Caroline listening to him, mouth a little tight, and an obscure desire to wound and expose possessed him. 'Herbivorous *Guardian*-reading stuff,' he went on, 'but with a nasty little hard, illiberal centre. None so naturally fascist, when it comes down to it, as the sanctimonious lefty. Particularly the female of the species.'

'My dear old chap,' said Tom heartily. 'How wonderful for once these days to find myself in such agreement with you. What has come over you?'

'I think,' said Jerome clearly, in measured tones, 'that you both sound like Genghis Khan. Shut up, Dad, for God's sake.'

'Yes, and *you* stop it, Dad, too,' said David, not to be outdone, adding in a furious undertone – 'Leave Mum alone.'

'You were having a go at her yourself a moment ago,' Joe muttered back angrily, under cover of another conversation hastily started by Mary and Caroline.

'That's quite different,' David retorted witheringly. 'And you know it.'

He was, Joe knew, right.

Yes, I did want, long ago, to join Caroline's club, that exclusive club that was and is hers by birthright, so naturally that she herself is still unaware of belonging to it. She imagines herself, on the basis of minute differences such as reading *The Times* rather than the *Telegraph* and preferring Habitat mock-Victorian sofas to Harrods neo-Georgian ones, to be 'quite different from Mummy'. She does live in London, yes, I grant her that; she does dwell in a city in contradiction to that deep, deep anti-urban fantasy-rural snobbery with which her club is imbued. But that's mainly because *I* will not live anywhere but London. And in any case the vast, green, residential sprawl of London is hardly 'city-living' by the standards of any Continental metropolis. Good God, we even have muddy wellingtons in the lobby by the garden door, rabbits, an apple tree, bonfires, an asparagus bed . . . 'WASPS', people like Caroline and her family are called in America. That the term has never really caught on in Britain is simply an indication of how extraordinarily pervasive and dominant the British, upper-class Anglo-Saxon Protestant culture is: it does not need a name.

Yes, I wanted to submerge myself in all that, to become one with it. The disappearance for ever of little Josef Buchsbaum. His annihilation, not by cyanide and fire but by assimilation.

'My wife doesn't understand me' indeed – the classic excuse for infidelity. There are no excuses for me because that was the very reason I married her: that she deeply did not understand by life what I did. I was safe from discovery with her.

Safe for years, that is, till the banked fires of alien subversion began to burn. When we married she took over my life competently, devotedly – and, yes, I wanted her to. It was years before I noticed, and then became haunted by, the similarity in English between the phrase 'took over his life' and 'took his life'.

If I am dying, then, as I sometimes feel, I am dying not of evil but of healthy, good, benign elements I once confusedly saw as curative. As in Karl Kraus's convoluted remark about something being the very spiritual disease 'of which is purports to be the cure'. I – we – are dying of the selfsame things we used to pride ourselves on: tolerance, restraint, rationality . . . I would have added 'morality' but cannot of course add that now. Or for years, actually.

'*The Gods are just, and of our pleasant vices –* ' But vice would be simple. It's of our pleasant *virtues* that the Gods have made instruments to plague us, or at any rate me. My pleasant optimism, my pleasant innocence. My pleasant faith in the theoretically 'good marriage'. It is that, no obviously selfish vice, that turns out eventually to be the emotional trap, the failure in courage and integrity . . . Or does it?

Sometimes, these days, I want to detach myself from all this just as passionately as I ever wanted to belong – But no, that isn't quite right. Let me be precise. It isn't so much that I want to as that I feel – hope? – dread, yes dread, that I *am doing so*. The abyss is there.

Is this week to come a surcease, a help, a restorer (as we both, separately, hope)? Or is it merely the last good time? Does it, as I feel in my bones, presage some further crisis, disaster – row? accident? – that will finally blast us apart?

Or weld us inexorably together, like fire, forever?

What rot, as Jerome would say: God wot rot. You're over-tired, over-emotional and self-indulgent. You are a middle-aged man who takes on too much at work and too much privately as well. You have had too long a day, too much to eat this evening and also probably too much to drink. You ought to put that damned stupid secret Notebook of yours away and stop thinking of yourself as Cyril

Connolly, and make up your mind just to enjoy the next few days properly for what they are. What else, for God's sake, is life but that?

3

The first morning dawned, as Tom Lovell had predicted, in mist: yesterday's piled snow was already pitted with drips from the eaves. But the genial elder statesmen among the ski instructors, marshalling classes outside the ski school with flags and a whistle, assured everyone that the day was 'luffly on zer mountain'.

'I like the old ones,' said Lisette happily: she and David had insinuated themselves together into his class. 'They don't take it all so terribly seriously as the younger ones, do they? Last time I went skiing my instructor was so frightfully solemn and sort of bullying that I ended up quite miserable!'

'That chap looks to me more the sort who optimistically takes beginners up onto black runs and then has to fill them up with tea-and-rum to get them down again,' said Tom cheerfully.

'Oh surely not?' said Caroline at once. 'I mean – he's in *charge*.'

'Doesn't mean much – ' Tom was evidently about to embark on some sadistic tale, and Mary cut in:

'Well at least one would get the tea-and-rum. I agree with Lisette, it's supposed to be fun, dammit. Thank God I'm so old, experienced and lazy these days that I need never have another lesson.'

Tom said he might 'invest' in a private lesson tomorrow – 'to rub the rust off me. Going to go shares in it with me, Joe?'

Joe said he might. In fact he felt as Mary did.

Caroline, stoic, signed up for a full course of lessons, as she did every time. Years ago she had stopped trying to follow the other three, though they always politely invited her to. I will *not*, she said to herself, be a burden on them. It irritated her the way they, and Joe particularly who really ought to have known better, urged her every year to attempt the runs they enjoyed, speciously telling her they were 'really

52

quite easy'. Easy! Those terrifyingly narrow, perpendicular slopes, strewn with rocks, where one false move . . .

'I know my place,' she said firmly, walking beside Jerome. 'And it isn't with the high flyers.'

'Nor mine,' said Jerome mournfully. 'I seem to land in the same class every year. I never get any better. Fact is,' he added, 'I suppose I make such a perfectly marvellous rabbit that there's no real incentive for me to improve to join the hares.'

'Oh I do sympathize,' said Caroline, considerably cheered. Perhaps they would get allocated to the same class? She would feel so much better with Jerome there to understand, as children did, and protect her against all the other people half her age.

To reach the ski school and the lift installations they had had to cross the main railway line that bisected the small mountain village. At that hour in the morning the level crossing was crowded with people going liftwards, but as Joe and Mary, lagging behind the others, had reached it, bells began to ring, the space was cleared, barriers descended, and there was a brief wait while a long-distance train came by. It went slowly, just leaving the station, waiting to pick up speed till the crossing should be passed. Passengers, fresh from their night in the sleepers, stood by the windows enjoying the picturesque scene, *The Skiers* by Breughel, while the skiers ignored the train as an unseemly eruption from a lower world. Except for Joe. His eyes followed it.

'You know where that train's going?' he said to Mary as its noise dwindled and the barriers swung up again.

'No idea – why?'

'It's going to Vienna. And at the end of this week I shall take off my skis and get onto it as well, not onto that one but onto an evening one – and go to sleep. And when I wake up in the morning I shall be arriving in the city.'

'Clever,' said Mary admiringly. 'I'd no idea this extra convenience for you existed in Heiligenhof. I supposed you'd have to spend hours on a bus going down to Innsbruck or somewhere first. Is this the main reason we're all in Heiligenhof this year, Joe? You are a sly old thing.'

'No I'm not,' he said in confusion, feeling that she had understood more in his words than he had intended. 'I swear, it was basically Caroline who picked this place out of the brochures. And you all said it looked nice.'

'Well you must have been delighted when you realized it was actually on the main railway. What a piece of serendipity.'

'Indeed,' he said, not looking at her.

Seeing that train made him irrationally happy. The obscure terror of the night-journey to come evaporated; instead, the iron line appeared to him that morning as a cord linking him already with his destination. His ultimate destination, that was.

Ultimate?

And then he forgot the train again, or rather submerged it in a general physical happiness. As the ski instructor had claimed, it was brighter up on the mountain, the mist all below them. He, Tom and Mary, having waved the others off to their respective groups and argued together over a map, went up very high. Cabin lift gave way to chair lift and then to a steep drag. Up and up they went, into ever bluer, thinner air, ever more crystalline snow. Clinging to the T-bar with Mary beside him – Tom, at sixteen stone, usually took a bar to himself behind them – Joe felt that they could go on rising and rising indefinitely into inexhaustible further sunlit, icing-sugar worlds.

On the first, brief, very steep slope down from the drag, Tom fell heavily, to his surprised disgust.

'You all right?' Joe, following him down, circled in front of him, momentarily afraid that this heavy, middle-aged man had mislaid all his skill and was about to roll right down the mountain.

'Of course I'm fucking all right. Go on, go on – I'll catch you up – '

'*Oh* dear,' said Mary, wiping her goggles as they waited

for Tom, a hundred metres down on the first plateau – he had taken his time about rising and readjusting his bindings: 'I knew this would happen. He *will* spend fifty-one weeks of the year driving to work and eating business lunches and falling asleep over the telly in the evenings, and then he expects to come out here and snap right into the form he used to have twenty years ago.'

'So tiresome and childish, chaps.'

'Quite.'

But when Tom rejoined them, skiing with a stylish carefulness now, he was determinedly nonchalant again. Joe relaxed once more, and began to enjoy himself passionately and consciously. He discovered again that whatever his fuddled mind had refused to recall, straining in the night, wondering 'Can I cope? Can I get there?' his legs did not forget. Bodies do not forget. When I die, he thought, my legs will still know how to ski, this other painless, intoxicating flying. Just as I suppose my hands will still know how to type, or play the piano, how to change a baby's napkin, or – by then all knowledge will have become irrelevent. But so much is already irrelevant, so many dormant facts, reflexes and memories curled up inside one's skull, all there but slumbering and, if not roused and disinterred, slumbering more and more deeply, stiffening and ossifying till sleep at the last becomes coma.

Whoever said one should live every day of one's life as if it might be the last got it right. But then when the next day dawns, and the next . . .

Having negotiated another descent and come out on to a broad mountain plain, with the brilliant sun in his eyes and burning his cheeks and his grease-smeared lips, he allowed himself the luxury of turning to Tom and saying, 'Anna would love it here.'

'Anna – ?'

'Anna Morley.'

'Oh. Yes.' Tom bent over one boot, fussing with the binding again, grunted heavily. He heaved himself up, splayed round to face in the opposite direction – an old-fashioned skill on his long, old-fashioned skis – and said:

'Yes. Anna. Will you get her out here, do you think?'

Jesus Christ, thought Joe; I didn't know Tom understood a thing, and yet . . . Taking fright at Tom's perhaps innocent and general remark, he said at random:

'No, no, she's in Manchester. Aidan's sick, and naturally she doesn't want . . . I say, Tom, I feel a bit strange. Sort of light-headed. I wonder if it's the altitude? Maybe we should have thought twice before coming right up here on the first day?'

'Yeah, I expect it's the altitude,' said Tom, with kindly lack of concern. 'Jesus, this fucking *binding* . . .'

Live each day as if it were the last. Each time together as if it were the only time and must be sufficient unto itself and for everything. That's what Anna and I have done these past years. Or I have. I cannot speak for her – I never have been able to. I think, perhaps, she lives more naturally on the frontier of time than I do. She told me once that she never thinks much about the future, and her tone was one of faint reproach and squeamishness, as if to think about the future was a recognized weakness, slightly indecent, avoided by sensible people in the same way that nostalgia for the past is to be avoided.

I envy her. And yet, in spite of being like this, is Anna any more free than I am? Not really. She makes an impression on people of elusiveness and independence, a cat person is Anna. Yet in reality something seems to keep her attached to a place, a set of circumstances . . . Perhaps that is like a cat too. She lives with Aidan in that great stone house outside Manchester; I always think of it as a cold house, though in fact it is efficiently heated. I suppose I think of it like that because it is so much the *sort* of oversized English house which is traditionally cold, a place of draughty hallways, distant bathrooms, oases formed by small electric fires and hot water bottles. It's a far larger, grander house than people like the Morleys would have in London, but of course the north is like that. Beastly, alien place, full of people priding themselves (as Anna once put it) on being rude and boring to show how real they are. Of course, not being rude or boring herself, she'd never say that to their faces or even, I suspect, to Aidan. For the north isn't alien to him, for all his Wykhamist manner: he comes of one of those northern shipping families. A chair at Manchester University probably seems to him the natural resting place for his career, so there, perforce, Anna too has taken her teaching skills, her gift with languages, grateful (in these times) for whatever lowly assistant lectureship she can get. But it isn't the place you'd expect to find her in, not that four-square pillared house, not that vast, revolting urban agglomeration . . . But then, where would I expect to find Anna? In a small apartment with nineteenth-century furniture in Paris or some other European city? In an eyrie in New York? Somewhere simple overlooking the Mediterranean or Adriatic Sea? But if I were to cite any of these to Anna she would say I was being sentimental, that I am merely reciting the places she and I have been in together, for a few days at a time, times without past or future; that place is not so important to her, that she can live anywhere. With a touch of obsessionalism, I think, she maintains that. The exile's defence. '*All places that the eye of heaven visits . . .*'

Years and years ago, when Anna and Aidan were in Cambridge, we saw them quite often. They used to come up to London. Caroline was very keen, in those days, on having people 'round' for Sunday lunchtime drinks, and on giving carefully selected dinner parties with elaborate food over which she toiled unnecessarily for days beforehand. The same devotion with which, a few years later, she expended her energies on neighbourhood street parties, making twenty quiches on one Saturday till her hands trembled and she was too tired to enjoy the party herself: the deliberate creation of burdens in the interest of some unspecified obligation, the very opposite of freedom. For *having fun* is never, apparently, the point of anything for Caroline. We didn't, it seemed, organize those mock-democratic street parties years ago in order to have fun but 'because it's rather expected of us, isn't it? I mean, we are in a position to'. We didn't, in the early days, invite Aidan and Anna all the way from Cambridge on a winter Friday night to eat laboriously home-made paté, *coq au vin*, potato croquettes and lemon mousse, so much because we wanted their company (that was somehow never discussed) but because we 'ought to see them again' and 'they would go well with the So-and-Sos'. (All that busy game of married life at which I too readily connived, yes, yes, I know.) If really pressed on the matter I suspect Caroline would have admitted that she felt the Morleys to be the sort of people we, as a couple (the Royal, marital 'we') *ought* to be friends with. The fact that Aidan and I, in spite of our joint, disparate intellectualism, had strangely little in common with each other, and that Caroline herself did not really, at the deepest level – I knew – like Anna at all, was excluded from her overall view of the matter. So that, when the Morleys did not invite us back very often, Caroline was genuinely a little hurt and indignant. Evidently, to her way of thinking, once you had begun to exchange hospitality with someone, an unspoken rule held both parties to that contract forever. Scenting the growth of one of Caroline's unnameable grievances, I tried to defuse it:

'Oh, I don't think Aidan cares for people much, you know, except when they're in exactly the same line as himself and he can argue about Wittgenstein with them. And Anna – well, you know Anna: she's got her own career, and she's never been much of a one for housekeeping anyway.'

It wasn't true. Anna may be impatient of guest towels or even fresh sheets for guests, but, when she makes the effort, she's a far better natural cook than Caroline will ever be – Caroline, who measures everything and is surrounded by electric mixers and peelers and timers. And anyway, as soon as I'd said it, I knew that 'Anna's got her own career' hadn't been a tactful phrase. For Caroline, then and for many years, did no job outside the home, being deeply engaged in what she was *just* sophisticated enough not to refer to as 'the more important job of bringing up the children'. She was deeply defensive about this, I don't know quite why, speaking at times as if having children was some eccentric and self-sacrificing minority cult on which she and I had decided in spite of unspecified easier alternatives. In fact, of course, at the age we were in those prosperous late-1960s, everyone all round us was having children. The only people who didn't were Aidan and Anna Morley.

'Oh, I don't think Anna cares for children,' Caroline used to say, dismissively and – was it? – resentfully. Evidently Anna was already, even then, her enemy, though I don't think she knew it.

I thought Anna did care for children, in fact. Oh, she was bored, as what unencumbered adult wouldn't be, by all the ritualized paraphernalia of British childhood which seemed so important to Caroline – the insistence on children's tea, on baths every night, on never going on holiday anywhere where the food might not be 'suitable' – but Anna talked to our children and they responded to her. How old can they have been when she told them that story they enjoyed so and which made Caroline so obscurely cross? Six and four? Something like that. Anna had appeared on her own to spend the night with us – passing through London, it seemed, on her way back from some Continental relative – and both Jennifer and David clamoured for her 'story about the two naughty children playing in that garden'. Amused and tired, a little detached, still with the patina of some European city on her like a stylish foreign garment, she finally identified what they were talking about and retold the tale. It unrolled gradually with apparently *ad hoc* embellishments, detours and local references, and it was only as it neared its climax that Caroline and I realized it was the story of the Fall.

I was vastly entertained. Caroline, for some reason I could not then fathom but can now, was not. She pretended afterwards that it was because, having brought the children up in a dedicated agnosticism and deliberately chosen for them a primary school where they would not be 'indoctrinated with tales about Jesus' we surely 'didn't want their heads filled with Old Testament rubbish'. I was baffled, because I knew that even Caroline was not such a prig as all that. Anyway, Anna's version – complete with an irascible, Mr McGregorish Old-Gentleman-in-Charge and two naughty children who, having stolen the apples, said things like '*She* made me do it' and 'It's not fa-air!' – was so transformed from its Biblical original as to be almost unrecognizable. Only later, thinking about it, did it dawn on me that Caroline disliked and feared Anna's story for the same reason that I liked it – that is, because, in spite of its transformation, David at any rate had got the central point of it.

'It was lucky, really, those children *did* eat those apples,' he managed to bring out, after several false starts. 'Because . . . if they hadn't of . . . then they wouldn't never have got out of the garden and would have had to stay there always!'

He looked justifiably triumphant at his philosophical conclusion, and Anna kissed him and said: 'That's right.'

Jennifer looked more dubious. Though older than David she was more obedient than he was by nature, and there seemed to be an obscurely immoral element in the story which was evidently bothering her. She clearly wanted to say, but didn't, 'It's not fa-air . . .' It was her great phrase in those days, poor little usurped elder child, and by incorporating it in the web of the story Anna had been teasing her.

Anna gave Jennifer a perfunctory hug too, then stretched in front of the fire like a satisfied cat. 'Oh, by the way,' she said after a long moment, 'who told you Adam and Eve were children?'

Our two children looked at her, lips parted, pondering deeply on this revolutionary question. They were silent. Anna said:

'I never *said* they were children, did I? . . . Perhaps they were two grown-ups all the time.'

After another silence Jennifer said disapprovingly, 'They couldn't of been.'

'Why not?'

'Because . . . Because grown ups don't steal apples.'

'Sometimes they do!'

'And grown-ups don't play in gardens,' said David, not to be outdone.

'Oh, but they do. We've got some lovely gardens in Cambridge that are just for grown-ups. With Old Gentlemen in Charge too, called things like Provosts and Masters.'

'Come on you two,' said Caroline loudly. 'I said it would be bedtime when Anna had finished her story and now it is.' In the general rumpus of toy collection and admonition that surrounded the children's preliminary moves on the elaborate bath-bed programme, she managed to say to Anna:

'Anna, dear, stories are fine – you tell them so well – but I do rather wish you wouldn't go in for these cute grown-up jokes over the children's heads. It bothers them rather.'

Recalling all this now, Caroline's unease seems to me so transparent, the symbolism of the story so obvious, that I can hardly believe it all happened before, years before . . . Yet I know it did. Extraordinary as it seems to me now, no glimpse of the future was revealed to me that evening in our drawing room.

In the years after that Anna came with us and the Lovells on two skiing holidays, the first time with Aidan who was an adamant non-skier but used the week to sit in the hotel writing a long article on semantics. He was not very good company for us nor we, after a day in the snow, for him. (Mary wickedly christened him, out of his hearing, 'The Spectre at the Feast'.) The next year the experiment was not repeated. By that time the Morleys had moved to Edinburgh and, for the next few years, we saw little of either of them.

No, it's no good, I cannot now trace the exact route by which Anna came into my life again, and then – and then – Can one ever trace such things clearly, afterwards? *'Ce n'est que le premier pas qui coute.'* But that was not true, in any sense, for me and Anna. She was not my 'first' any more than I was hers. In those years when, incredible as it seems now, we never saw each other, I had already had a number of minor affairs. What else can I call them? I know that the stilted term is an indictment of me as much as of the unfortunate girls; and if I add, by way of excusing myself, that it was just too easy, that also brands me as a selfish, empty philanderer. But the simple fact is that those clandestine adventures had no transforming effect, no one became for me what Anna has now become. Why Anna? I do not know. It just is so.

I think the Morleys were already in Manchester that time when she and I had lunch together at the Garrick; she had an idea for a book – never eventually written – that she wanted to discuss with me. She told me then that on that evening in our house, the time of the Adam and Eve story, when she had just arrived back from visiting an elderly aunt abroad, it had not been just an aunt that she had been visiting.

Had Caroline, more astute for once than I was, picked something of this up from Anna's manner? Had her annoyance about the story been because of this – the citadel of family life threatened by such a subversive influence?

I asked Anna if 'it' was over now, and she said yes, it had been awful – really agonizing – but it was now over.

I said I was 'sorry', meaning I suppose something generalized and conventional like 'I'm sorry if you've been suffering' or 'I'm sorry if you and Aidan aren't happy together', and she shrugged and said after a while:

'Oh but . . . it isn't always the person who means most to one who becomes a lover.'

At the time, I found that remark of hers obscurely cheering and perhaps flattering. Now it comes back to me with a slightly bitter taste.

It was after that again – oh, but more than two years after, Jennifer was already in her teens – that at last Anna and I met in a foreign city. I was at the Frankfurt Book Fair and she had been at a language seminar in Mannheim and came on to Frankfurt to see a German co-editor of some academic journal. We had, on that occasion, planned nothing, manoeuvred nothing: it was as if (it seemed to me afterwards in myopic elation) we had both been subconsciously waiting all those fallow years for this time to come of its own accord. And so it came. And so – and so –

And so what? What then? In youth and in novels people who fall in love commonly alter the whole course of their lives to stay together. But that is youth, and novels. We were neither of us young any more. And, as Anna says, novels, with their obsessional, artificial themes to do with guilt and retribution, that pattern-making that the children used maddeningly to call 'fa-airness', are a thoroughly misleading guide to the real nature of life.

And in any case, is Anna in love with me? *Does* Anna fall in love? It isn't a term she uses, and perhaps just as well. Perhaps, as she would say, that's a novelist's term too. Perhaps. I tell myself that, sometimes.

Once, when we were saying one of our goodbyes – in Frankfurt, was it, or in Paris or New York? – I said something about it being painful. I suppose I wanted her to say something like 'Yes, it hurts me too most awfully. Oh darling . . .' I wanted her to cry. She didn't contradict me, but somehow her response was quite other. 'Of course it's painful,' she said, almost reproachfully. 'One knows that from the beginning. You must have known it would be.' As if I were soft, fussing on my own account, a spoilt adolescent who had not yet understood the nature of life, of the human condition.

Defensive, I tried to explain to her that I was complaining not just of my own pain but trying to empathize with what I supposed or hoped was hers. I ran into difficulty at that point, not knowing quite how to say I hated the idea of her going back to that northern, alien place, to that house with the pillars and the semicircle of gravel, its drawing room and morning room and cavernous kitchen and Aidan's dressing room – to Aidan himself, shut away in his study, writing late, his impenetrable good manners, his occasional devastating sarcasm, his fundamental self-sufficiency. On his mother's side, I believe, his forebears were district collectors and governors of remote Indian or African provinces, and that, perhaps, is what Aidan himself is equipped to be. I see him dressed for dinner in the bush, bent over a camp table in the light of a petrol lamp, doggedly translating Thucydides (or whatever), stoically ignoring the exotic insects that hum and bump in the yellow circle of light: the Burra Sahib, the Boss-man, eternally alone. I have seen him, two or three times, brush Anna aside as if she were an importunate insect, and I have seen the look on her face. It is not so much that he is happy, Aidan, as that he always wins by not minding if he is happy or not – by not seeing life in those terms. He too, perhaps, has formed the opinion that life is inevitably painful and so what? – that view against which I feebly, rebelliously, struggle.

Anna said to me on that or another occasion, speaking a little as if she were comforting a child:

'Sometimes, you know, one thinks one is upset because of *this* or *that* or if only someone else would be different, when really what one is minding is the nature of life itself, the way things are, the pain that just *is there*.'

Possibly she was trying to tell me that life with Aidan was not really so bad, that I shouldn't blame him for anything or, by extension (a taboo topic between us but she must have thought about it) seek to lay the blame for my own situation on Caroline. But, if so, I was not then in any mood to receive her message. Then – what? Five – three – years ago, I was still deeply involved in that compulsive lover's daydream in which my loved one's husband was finally such a brute to her that she left him, and that Caroline, coincidentally, conveniently and painlessly disposed of herself.

A rapid leukaemia, perhaps, through which of course I would devotedly support her. Thus, in her last illness, she would be reinstated, paradoxically given back to me again in her original purity by the certitude and imminence of death, enabling me to love her once again, leaving no stain of guilt or reproach behind. And afterwards I would freely take Anna by the hand and we could walk off together into a brand new life – ah, the mirage of the New Life, shining and simple and easy, with none of the accumulated detritus of the old one, the intolerable litter of years . . . And everyone, including the children, would be pleased with us.

God wot rot, as Jerome would say.

In reality there are no such painless get-outs, no completely new lives. Nor is rapid, easy death in hitherto healthy middle-aged women that common. No, if Caroline were to get 'anything', as one evasively says, it would be something slow and nasty and uncertain and real, dammit, real, and I should myself be racked by distress, anxiety, conflicting feelings, guilt – *guilt* . . . Anna, remorselessly clear-sighted, says that guilt is commoner in fiction (and in psychoanalysis, that other literary construct) than it is in real life, but I'm not so sure. I believe she is thinking of sexual guilt, and I would agree with her there, but there are other far worse forms of betrayal, and anyway Anna has her own quite separate reasons for not being interested in guilt . . . No, I don't want even to try the Caroline-dying fantasy on these days: my mind slithers, cowardly, away from it. Particularly since it has become fashionable to wonder if cancer isn't caused, in some large measure, by stress: partisan articles in the Sunday papers, contention about Positive Thinking, opinions in the guise of statistics – just the sort of thing Caroline herself gets very involved with.

Stress, in any case, has many other possible manifestations, most of them not lethal.

If Caroline . . . If Caroline were, oh God, to fall to bits in one of those awful non-specific ways in which people, and particularly women, do fall to bits in middle life, those few who, in the confusion, got to know or guess about Anna would no doubt lay the matter solidly at her door and mine. The Lovells, my secretary at work, the children just possibly, oh God the unforgiving children . . . Even a year ago, punch-drunk with my own misbehaviour, I would have said they might be right: a banal, inglorious but all-too-common situation: husband deserts wife for newer love. Well, well, the wife was always too much *thus*, wasn't she, and the other woman so much *other*, but gosh how badly he's behaved . . . But now, recently, somehow, I don't see it like that any more. It is as if Anna is nothing whatsoever to do with Caroline, or with my marriage. It is, rather, as if Anna's and my association has always had a life of its own, long before we became lovers, and that that life will, regardless of other elements, follow its own separate, insulated course until, until – until what?

This appointment in Vienna. We've never met there before – never been as far east as that. Back to our joint origins: it seems apposite, we even joked about the suitability of it when we made our private arrangement. Why, then, do I now dread it? What am I dreading? A crisis, no doubt. A climax, and explosion, an ending, a beginning – I don't know.

In their large and heterogeneous class of post-beginners, Caroline and Jerome were, once again, being taught parallel turns. She, in an access of energy and optimism, decided that this year she really would make significant progress; she stayed close behind the instructor and glowed when he praised her. Jerome, intent rather on enjoying himself harmlessly and keeping out of the instructor's way, stayed at the back of the wavering line. Presently, as temporary star pupil, Caroline was sent to join him, and the instructor beckoned nearer to him the White Mouse from their chalet who, even by Caroline and Jerome's modest standards, was clearly no skier.

'Isn't it sad,' said Jerome to Caroline as they waited for a chair lift, 'that, by Wednesday, we won't be the goodies of the class any longer. The others will have forged ahead, and he'll be disappointed in us because we haven't learnt to do turns any quicker.'

It seemed dreadful to Caroline that a boy the age of her own son should be so resigned to his rôle.

'Oh *no*, Jerome,' she scolded him. '*I* might say that but not you. At your age you'll inevitably go on getting better. And I know what you mean about some of them – that dark boy looks rather too good for us already, doesn't he, and I believe he's only been skiing once before, oh goodness – but what about that girl from our chalet, you've seen her?'

He smiled wanly, easing his goggles on his sun-reddening

nose, then dropping a stick and having difficulty retrieving it. When the children were younger, she remembered, it was always Jerome who got in a muddle with his equipment, forgot to do up the cleats on his boots or alternatively did them so tight he couldn't undo them, and – once – lost a ski on a chair lift. She recalled his agonized face and gestures as he turned round to them from the swinging chair ahead, and Tom's stentorian bellow at her side 'Stop the lift! *Arrêtez!*' seeing as he did that his son would never extricate himself from a moving chair on one ski.

Joe, as the best skier present, had had to lend his own skis to Jerome to get him down the mountain. The missing ski was never recovered from the inaccessible gulf into which it had fallen, and no one had been pleased with poor Jerome.

Now, bracing themselves to get together into another chair lift – goodness, it was going *fast* – she beamed at him affectionately and said:

'Hang onto your skis!'

With a flurry and a heave, hearts pounding, they were safely installed. Then the lift stopped abruptly: the White Mouse, behind them, had apparently failed to make it; Caroline felt for her. Then the chairs continued on their ascent and she relaxed. She always enjoyed gratefully these interludes from the strain, when she was cast suddenly into a silent and dreamlike whiteness and need only sit there while precipices and abysses passed harmlessly below her.

But this time, rather than daydreaming, she had an impulse to use the ride to get emotionally closer to Jerome. She felt that, in spite of his deprecating, ironic air of detachment, he really was not happy. She was so fond of him, she said to herself – how could she not be, remembering him as a damp toddler, and as a six-year-old lecturing her on UFOs? – and she wished he would confide in her. Nothing particular. Anything.

But by and by an inspiration came to her, and she said:

'I'm so sorry you have to share a room with a stranger, Jerome. I'd have preferred – but never mind. I hope the chap you're with is all right?'

'Oh – you mean the Non-Scorer?' Jerome turned towards her a face ghastly with graveyard humour.

'The what? Who – ? I mean that young man who's really one of the party in the chalet next door. Isn't that who you're sharing with?'

'Yes, indeed it is. Oh, he's harmless enough, I suppose. I mean, he doesn't smell revolting or anything. But he came in really late last night.'

'Oh poor Jerome, did he wake you up?'

'No, no, I wouldn't have minded that, I'd just have gone off again. Anyway I was still reading. No, but do you know what he was on about?' Jerome's normally rather high voice reached a new pitch of incredulity and indignation. 'He was moaning like hell because he and that lot he's with had gone out drinking with some girls they met on the coach yesterday, but he *hadn't scored yet.*'

'You mean . . . ?' said Caroline, shrinking.

'Yes I do mean. He really thought, the idiot, that because he hadn't *scored* on the very first evening with some unknown girl he was being cheated of something. He carried on about it as if he was going to claim a rebate from the tour operator! Oh, he was a bit drunk I suppose. But *honestly*, I got the impression he thought that was what skiing holidays are *for*. I don't think he's been before.'

After a minute Caroline said:

'But goodness, Jerome, it isn't fair on you having to share with someone like that. Why, he might even try to bring . . .' No, awful thought, better not to say it. 'I wonder if we couldn't speak to the chalet girls – to that yellow girl who seems to be in charge – ask her if she can't make some more suitable arrangement.'

'Oh, please don't bother!' Jerome's grin became more ghastly. 'I expect by and by I'll get hooked on this frightful guy! Like *Coronation Street*, you know. Or *Dallas*, rather. I'll give you regular bulletins.'

She could not reply, as the lift was reaching the upper station.

★

. . . And if it is Anna driving me apart from Caroline, sowing destruction in our life, why, these days, do I keep finding myself thinking not of her but of my father?

I believe I dreamed of him again last night. Him – or was it Ted Litvak? Now I try to recall it, I'm not quite sure. But it does not seem important if it were he in my dream or my actual father, *mein Vater, Papa – Paperl*, my sister used to call him, that ubiquitous and ridiculous Viennese diminutive applied even to its cathedral: *Steffel*. Little Father . . . Give me a small buncherl . . . Where's the keyerl? . . . Wait a momenterl . . . Our mother rather objected to *Paperl:* I imagine she thought it common.

In dreams, different persons are conflated, laid one upon another like transparencies to create an Ur-Person that has the essential qualities of both. That, perhaps, is one of the things that is meant by there being truth in dreams.

But I would maintain (more contra-Freud, this) that what you don't dream is as important as what you do. For years – for decades – I never dreamed of my father at all. Or, for that matter, my mother or my sister or any of my numerous relations. It seems extraordinary now, but it was so. Just as if, that day in June 1939, the whole lot had fallen through a trap door into an abyss. Though perhaps it was rather *I* who had fallen through the trap door, like Alice falling down the rabbit hole, and had emerged into another country.

I did occasionally, when I was a child in England, dream of our small black dog. Yes, I did dream of Mitzi – Mitzerl – I believe I missed her rather. Till my kind foster parents acquired a terrier for me: then she faded. Some things, evidently, are safe to dream about, whilst others –

It seems to me too that occasionally in my dreams as a schoolboy my home appeared. Not our actual apartment in Günthergasse, behind the Votifkirche in a block that has since been rebuilt (a few perilous stone-throws, I now know, from Freud's niche in Berggasse): that apartment, with its heavy divans and console tables that, in the end, were to be the millstones that dragged my parents down to their death, did not reappear again till I was married and Caroline and I

69

were furnishing our own home; then I was highly disconcerted by it. But in my dreams as a growing youth Vienna was quite often there. Only it had ceased somehow to be *my* Vienna, but became just an archetypal city of high, foreign buildings and crowds of people in dark clothes: a metaphoric city, a concentrated dream one rather than a specific one, a place of meeting and parting where I believed I knew people but where I searched for a familiar face among all those hatted, overcoated, hurrying people and did not find one.

But this grainy, black-and-white vision, like a pre-war film, is itself suspect. There have been too many overlays, too much culture. My view differs from that of the small Viennese boy I once was, not only in its vantage point but being hopelessly, irretrievably educated. And I suspect those hurrying, dark-coated, dream crowds with their old-fashioned Homburgs, felt cloches or baggy caps, '*crowds of people walking in a ring*': I think they come from literature, not from memory (though Ted Litvak, with his gentle predilection for Jung as opposed to the didactic Viennese hobgoblin would counter that with 'But literature *is* memory, Joe – collective memory'). More precisely, I suspect that they owe themselves in part to those film clips of European Jews being marched off somewhere in powdery snow, hats on heads, suitcases and children by the hand, tramlines under foot. We have all seen those clips so often, going round and round in the projector of time, anniversary after anniversary, churned out again and again till meaning has been squeezed from them. The once heart-rendingly precise images have been worn, by sheer repetition, to smudgy silhouettes, hieroglyphs of horror. We review them as one repeats a litany – or a prayer in Hebrew – as a ritualized gesture of respect: this real power to move is exhausted.

Even those *other* pictures, the last ones, that so disconcerted the world when they first appeared on the newsreel screens in 1944, those naked, emaciated, piled-up bodies – even those have now, by time and exposure, been rendered stereotypic, dried shells of meaning.

1944. I was twelve. Going to the cinema regularly with

friends from school, just too old, anyway, to be protected from knowing. But, even so, my life in England had, like that old life in Vienna, been so generally protected that I took a long time to put two and six million together, to understand . . . Nor was I alone in this. The resistance on the part of those not immediately involved towards comprehending the full enormity of what had taken place was formidable. And naturally no one wanted to encourage me, in my school blazer, to think too hard about the matter and draw too precise conclusions. So it was a long time, years even, before I did.

When I did, I became afraid ever to look at those last pictures, for the particular and cowardly reason that I was afraid I might recognize someone. I could not actually remember what my parents had looked like, and they did not then appear in dreams. But I had their photos, proper photos that had come with me to England in my suitcase, put there no doubt by my mother; she and my father small in oval frames, looking uninvolved, benign and overdressed. Not doomed. Not anyone, really. And I could remember my sister clearly.

Only when many more years had elapsed did I begin to understand that there was no question anyway of recognizing one individual among the unrecognizable, piled heaps, and that that indeed was the heart of the matter. Individuality itself, from a culture where the individual, in all his intricate, talented, ambitious wholeness was so important, had been annihilated: reduced to smoke, dust, conjectural statistics . . . nothing.

So really I cannot make any connection between the dark figures hurrying in a city that have so long been there for me, and my actual father as he appeared again last night: father-figure, Ted-figure, mild but slightly intimidating, genial but making me feel guilty, yes guilty. (For what? For leaving him? For having secrets from him?) He admonishes me in German, and I do not listen properly so do not understand.

But the general tenor of my dream is not threatening. I

think we are going on a picnic – him, and presumably my
mother and sister and various other indeterminate relations.
And this is entirely plausible, because indeed my early childhood, in so far as I remember it at all, seems to have been
full of such pleasures: spring picnics in the Prater, *Frühling
im Prater*, long tram rides out to Grinzing and Sievering,
summer and autumn trips in an aunt's motorcar into the
Wienerwald: a low sun dappling on the beech trees and their
reddened leaves like the picture in my mother's bedroom.
But in any case the town itself was full of gardens. Far from
being for me in extreme youth a city of high buildings and
strangers, Vienna was an extraordinarily safe place, where
I was constantly being protected by mufflers or sunhats,
accompanied by concerned, indulgent adults, carried whenever I was tired, never left alone even for half an hour, free
to play among the great rocky outcrops of furniture in a flat
that in my memory is enormous, plied with interminable
family meals and inter-meal treats in which cream figures
frequently . . . Or am I here again inventing? Literature
intruding again with the celebrated whipped cream of Viennese coffee, the chocolate cakes from Demels and Sachers?
But no, I really do remember an uncle, even older than my
father, more of a grandfather-figure to me I suppose, who
took me sometimes to the coffee house with him on Sundays
and let me spoon the cream from the top of his hot chocolate.
He was 'dieting', so he had only a single helping of cream on
top, not the double he would naturally have had otherwise.
(Young children are rarely surprised by anything grown ups
do, but as Onkel Gustaf's cream amused my parents and my
sister, I conserve it solemnly as my one surviving remembered example of the jokes that were surely an integral part
of our comfortable family life.)

My father was older than many people's fathers: I think I
was aware of that, even in a place and at a time when men
still in their twenties assumed the bearing and the waistcoats
of the middle-aged. There was poverty in Austria then,
between the wars: I remember, or think I remember, beggars
on the streets, lantern-jawed men with caps and mufflers

raucously peddling wooden toys, Bohemian glass balls and frightening *Fasching* masks. To be stately of bearing, fleshy, slightly ponderous in manner was then in Central Europe, as in a Third World country today, a sign of wealth and breeding. *La bonne bourgeoisie, Bürgertum* . . . Men, and women, knew the age they had reached, did not lose themselves in a wilderness of youth unnaturally prolonged.

All the same, my father was old to have a child as young as I was: he was in his mid-forties when I was born. My mother was younger, but still approaching forty. And as he was the youngest of his family my aunts and uncles on his side were older again, their own children nearing adulthood. Even my sister was seven years older than I was: I assume my parents were either hyper-cautious or not very fertile. I was the collective baby of that whole, large, well-satisfied, upwardly mobile tribe, and no doubt I thrived on it. I know that, young as I was, I had a confused but vaguely pleasant impression that I was the child of people of consequence and that life held good things for me.

Though solid and middle-aged my father was active. Not for him the double portions of cream of his elder brother or the lovingly nurtured minor ailments of his richest sister in her large house at Turkenschanzplatz. My evidence of this is that it was he who taught me to ski. Such a fact, though not startling, was, I now think, a little unusual for someone of his class and background. He and I used to take a tram up to the miniature snowy slopes of the Wienerwald on winter Sundays. I do not remember my sister coming with us. Perhaps she did not like skiing. Or perhaps – more likely, I think – such expeditions weren't considered so suitable for a daughter, however doted on. She would have been at home keeping Mama company, and thus learning (it was to be hoped) to be a good wife at some not-too-distant date to some nice young men of the right faith but without too much tiresome, lower-class orthodoxy.

No, I must admit, I am probably letting Literature intrude again: Literature or at any rate *post hoc* knowledge, gleaned from people like Ted Litvak who can recall what I can only sense and guess. But I do remember those skiing expeditions: indeed I believe I was back on one of them eventually in last night's dream, flying down some endless slope, frightened but elated with my father behind me like an irresistible force urging me downwards . . . *Paperl*. Little Daddy.

Grown-ups all smelt in my youth: can one genuinely claim to recall a smell? It is rather smells that recall other things for us. All I know is that, a few times in my life, when I have been near some heavy, elderly man, given to sweat, Turkish tobacco and eau de cologne rather than to dry cleaners and modern deodorants, I have felt a surge of wild, irrelevant emotion and nostalgia that I have subsequently, with vague incredulity, traced back to my father, to Papa.

Ted himself was not born in Vienna but in a small town in the eastern part of the ex-Austro-Hungarian Empire, then recently renamed Czechoslovakia. But, as he has said to me, 'In the sort of assimilated, middle-class Jewish family like mine, where Yiddish was forbidden, even, because German was the correct language, everyone looked towards Vienna. That was where life happened, where everyone hoped to go sooner or later. To us, it wasn't just a place, but a whole way of thought and social organization. There was a kind of cult called "Vienna", a belief called "Vienna" . . . When the empire went, that cult was all that was left.'

He has also said to me: 'Jews like my parents – and yours, I would guess – were so horribly *disappointed* when the Germans finally came for them. Well, "disappointed" is much too weak a word: I mean more like *enttäuscht*, with its sense of a degrading change for the worst, or the French *deçu*, with its double implication of disappointment and having been betrayed . . . I mean that they had believed themselves so assimilated, so Germanized in culture. When they were rounded up in the end like the poor Polish Jews of the world they had thought they had left behind them, it wasn't just death that had caught up with them but something worse: it was as if their whole idea of themselves and their identity was broken. *Kaput*.'

Ted speaks a number of languages: he learnt fluent English only in his twenties, as a refugee survivor, but it has become his main language, the one in which he teaches and writes, and he and I normally converse in it. Like our fathers before us, he and I are 'assimilated'.

When Czechoslovakia was invaded, Ted was a boy in his teens. Rounded up into a camp which must have been the first stop on the road to Auschwitz, he escaped, and then spent several years on the run, hiding alone in winter forests for weeks on end, stealing food in the fields, was chased away by hostile villagers, lived for a while with fairground gipsies, was rounded up again, escaped again . . . When I knew what this rotund, quiet, genial, almost fussy man in his sixties underwent, at an age when I was making a drama out of Higher School Certificate, the cricket team and girls, I quail with the knowledge of my own feebleness, of all I still have to learn. But I don't believe that I shall ever learn it.

On Ted's model, a mammoth crisis in youth – if you surmount it at all – allows you for ever to live out the rest of your life on some bright upland on the far side of fear. You have survived, however terribly. All the rest of life is a bonus and nothing more can touch you. You are free to re-invent pleasure in little things: short term hopes and desires, short stories.

Yes, but most people's lives aren't like that and never have been. In former times many lives, both men's and women's, must have consisted of a brief flowering, a short bright heroic summer – and then, quite soon, the dark; cold, sickness, no second chances. Today? Today crises mature more slowly, over a longer time span, and time itself becomes a daunting burden. We are, most of us, promised sixty, seventy, even eighty years of active life, but with no extra emotional equipment and stamina to deal with them. *Eighty*. Christ. How will I ever get there, across all that space? Strength, courage, belief – all fail me.

When Anna and I have spoken once or twice, fleetingly, circumspectly, of the fantasy of 'a life together some time',

I do not think either of us has envisaged anything like another quarter century, even in the most favourable and pain-free circumstances. I know I haven't. A few years, at most, is what I have in mind. A bonus-life, posthumous somehow. I cannot – really cannot – imagine anything more. I do not seem to have the equipment to do so.

I am physically strong and, as far as I know, healthy. Yet I am, in my mid-fifties, a decade older than my father was when he begat me. He himself was born in 1888. I do not know, can never know, the exact place nor date of his death. But it cannot have been later than 1944 and was very likely earlier. He must, in other words, have died at very much the age – perhaps the exact age – that I am now. Perhaps even today, in this wintry landscape, where I ski deliberately ahead of the others, ploughing on alone in the failing afternoon, down, down again into the rising mists of the valley floor – I am skiing unbeknown across his death-date in my own life, the day on which I become older than he was, the day he never saw.

Thomas Hardy writes of the anniversary of our future death coming round each year like a cold, hidden presence in the calendar. But what of the unmarked day on which we have *not* died, the date from which no forward, inherited maps exist?

I have no map for the rest of my life. Yes, that's what it feels like. All these years, it seems, I have been carrying, unknowingly, my father's map, aware of course that it was for another country but mindlessly imagining that the terrain was about right all the same: a route winding upwards via hard work, ambition and assimilation, marriage, two children (the girl older), friends, the pleasant, sunlit plateaux of what is called success and security. Ups and downs, of course, steep or tricky bits, places where one might fall, but all in all – and then, then what?

Then, in my father's map, a giant scar across the landscape, a scar called the Holocaust, inescapable whichever way you approach it, whatever skilled manoeuvre you adopt: a landslide, a precipice such as no skier can avoid, the map itself torn in two.

And it's no good you telling me, Mary or Ted or any other clever Dick who doesn't happen to be in a state of fear himself at this time, that I've got hold of the wrong map, an out-of-date one. It seems to be the only one I've got. It's that or no map at all, which is almost as frightening: Orpheus' unprecedented, trackless journey to the Underworld:

> 'Felsen waren da
> und wesenloser Wälder. Brücken über Leeres
> und jener grosse blinde Teich . . .'

> *But there were rocks*
> *and shadowy forests. Bridges over nothing*
> *And that immense, grey, unreflecting pool . . .*

I saw that pool from the chair lift above the glacier this morning. And I said to Mary, teasing her: 'Let's hope the cable doesn't break right here.' And she said: 'Oh, give over, Joe, for Christ's sake!'

But I *can't* give over, I can't, I only wish I could.

Ted himself has got it right. He knows. He said to me once:

'People like you and me, Joe, we can't hate the Holocaust – and we don't even have the option of being bored by it. Because it is part of us. We have internalized it. There is no escape. It is just there.'

But Ted has had his own holocaust, and, against all the odds, survived. I am still waiting for mine. Waiting.

4

On the Tuesday morning at breakfast Tom complained of a strained shoulder. Mary said she thought they'd all done rather a lot, yesterday, for the first day: personally her ankles were agony; she had taken against her boots which were very new and space-age – absolutely the best butter, the hire shop had assured her, and charged her extra for them, but she didn't like them and proposed to change them.

Joe, restless after waking early, and feeling that his own legs were only just beginning to be run in, envisaged half the morning disappearing while Mary went boot-hunting and Tom fussed over his shoulder, and then they drank coffee and argued over which route today would suit everyone's sensibilities. And, at this time of year with the days so short, mornings were the best time. He said he would go off on his own and meet them at one in the mountain café where they had had lunch the day before.

'The one by the hotel at the first lift-station?'

'That's right – the one with the round bar outside. I think I'll go up from there this morning and try that little black run up on the left. Then if I've time, I might ski over to St Wilhelm and come back on the Post-bus.'

'Oh, we thought of doing that, Dad,' said David. 'Shall we come with you?'

'I want to try the black run first,' Joe warned, not really wanting their company this morning but pleased that they wanted his, 'Look – this one.' He spread the map out. 'Are you sure you're up to it?' He really meant: are you sure Lisette's up to it? 'What about your class anyway?'

'There are too many of us: the instructor's splitting us into two and we're in the afternoon group.'

'I'm so relieved,' said Lisette. 'I don't really like Class all day – it takes the fun out of it.'

'Well, what about this black run? Perhaps you'd better do

it with me the first time, come to think of it.' He wanted
to protect her, her in her pink-and-blue snow suit.

'Dad, I'm not taking Lisette on a sneaky *black* run,' said
David with patient scorn. 'Like she said, she likes to enjoy
herself, but not face tests all the time. No, I just meant, shall
we come up in the lift with you and then peel off towards
the other valley?'

'Yes, of course. Eat up, and we'll go together.' He was
secretly amused at the transformation of David, who in the
past had always been wantonly adventurous and competitive
himself, into an indulgent husband-figure, modifying his
own skiing plans to suit the more delicate female require-
ments. No wonder Lisette seemed so happy with him. In a
sudden access of guilt Joe turned towards Caroline, busy a
little further down the table ingesting the 'good breakfast'
he knew she did not really want but believed she ought to
have to equip herself for the day.

'Are you all right, Caroline? Fancy a run with me later
today? You could meet us for lunch. I'm told there's some
nice wide open pistes between there and St Wilhelm.'

'Not today, thanks Joe,' she said pleasantly but firmly.
'Later in the week, perhaps. Jerome and I are fine in our
class for the moment, aren't we Jerome?'

'Yes . . . By the way, I don't see the White Mouse this
morning. She given up already, do you think?'

'I expect the Non-Scorer has got her in his clutches,' said
David, and he and Lisette collapsed into giggles.

(Caroline felt a tiny pang. Evidently Jerome's confidence
to her had already gone public, as it were, and was to be
one of this week's running jokes.)

'Not in our room, he hasn't,' said Jerome decisively. 'I
would have noticed. Even I.'

At the top of the cabin lift it was another sparkling morning.
Joe waved David and Lisette off on their way to the next
valley, thinking what an attractive pair they made. I hope
they're being careful, he thought, and then rethought – No,
dammit, I hope they're *not* being careful, not in bed anyway,

wherever else they are. At one level I profoundly wish that this handsome, healthy young couple could do as Nature intends and beget now, yes now, a child. In many other, older cultures they would be doing just that, blessed and encouraged by all concerned. A child – a grandchild – something for Caroline and me to live for, something beyond the abyss; what's wrong with that as a dream? Christ, it's better than my other, vain, sterile dreams, better by far than my nightmares –

But almost certainly, if his son and this girl found themselves going towards parenthood just yet there would be a general conspiracy that they were 'too young'. David's natural callousness of immaturity would be abetted, Lisette's own most secret dreams trampled on, the source of life trampled on – and he himself might not even be told about it. ('We won't tell Dad – he'd just be upset and cross.') God, he began to sweat at the very thought, and to struggle with an insane desire to go after them now, while he could still see them, and waylay them with solemn warnings mixed with fervent promises of support, if ever . . . Mad, they would think him. Quite mad.

He went to calm himself with a cup of coffee instead.

There were few people around the open-air bar at this hour. Yesterday at lunch time it had been crowded with ordinary skiers consuming beer, soup and toasted cheese, and he had hardly registered the hotel to which it was attached. Now, however, he saw that it was large, luxurious and certainly expensive: one of those curious one-purpose places halfway up a mountain, the apotheosis of the hermetic life of a ski resort. Yet the sprinkling of people seated at the bar at ten in the morning were not, now he came to look at them, skiers. They were women in fur coats and soft leather snow boots, the sort of people (he suddenly saw, with a sense of minor revelation) who go to ski resorts to be there rather than to ski.

He began to watch them. Basking in the glow of other people's exertion – or perhaps just in their own conspicuous wealth – they drank some sort of Schnapps and made arch, allusive conversation in German about last night's winnings at cards. They included the barman in their chat, calling him by his first name. Evidently they formed a group of their own. Were their husbands off, genuinely skiing, and due to return, adding their crude vigour, for lunch? Well, not in every case, he decided. Two men had now appeared, also fur-coated and soft-shoed, to a chorus of self-conscious welcome. They were younger than most of the women. One of them had just approached the woman nearest Joe and was embarking on a ritual of elbow-holding, finger-kissing and under-the-breath endearments which, Joe rather thought, was intended as much for public consumption as for private pleasure.

When the young barman brought him his coffee, Joe asked in soft German:

'Do these people really come and stay all the way up here and not ski?'

The waiter lowered his own voice and a look of curdling contempt came over his handsome actor's face.

'Rich Viennese ladies. Well, ladies – hmm! You see that one with the blonde mink and that little Yid slobbering over her?' (' – und jener kleiner Jud, der über sie so sabbert. Es ist zum Kotzen, kann ich Ihnen sagen.') 'Well, the day before yesterday he was with that other one over there, the fat dark bit . . . For the likes of them, this is a place to be seen in, and it's all a competition, everything is. Disgusting, I call it.'

Fearing to be told still more, Joe assented, and turned quickly to the ski map he fished out of his pocket.

You've always known such people exist, and can you blame the waiter for despising them? But why despise them, since they are harmless enough, not doing you any harm anyway, simply enjoying themselves in the only way they know.

'Rich Viennese'. The soft underbelly of that as of every other capital city. But particularly of Vienna. A 'melting pot' that, in practice, has cooked up all the ingredients of hatred, of discrimination. Where were these people's families in 1940? Useless to speculate. Such people have no past, they are of all time.

Imagine knocking back Schnapps this early . . . That's right, Joe, keep going, in a minute you'll have managed to feel sorry for them instead of affronted by them. The great Anglo-Saxon superiority-trick. Caroline, indeed, is awfully good at it. 'I'm sorry for Anna, really,' she once said in my hearing. And a mist of anger rose before my eyes, but I could say nothing.

Going up in a further lift, squinting down as he did to try to assess the steep run to which he was now committed, he thought: I wish I'd had Tom or Mary with me to 'place' those people in the café and make an instant joke of them. One needs defences first thing in the morning. He imagined to himself the loud conversation about knickerless-ness and score-keeping on which Tom, who had a line in gross pleasantries, would have embarked. But what line would Mary have taken? Mary was interested in women, he knew, and, while she was rude about present-day feminism ('them as can do and them as can't join women's groups') she said that she could well understand how women get driven into feminism or into other more traditional sources of spurious self-esteem.

'It's so hard to be a woman,' she had said to him once – when? He could not remember exactly, but knew it had been at a moment when she had seemed to him particularly successful and in charge of her own fate, and the remark, coming from her, had surprised him greatly.

'Discrimination?' he hazarded vaguely.

'No, soppy! You know I don't think that.' She blew smoke at him crossly. 'No, I mean – the inexorableness of change. The going on of time. Just those basic things.'

'Surely no harder for women than it is for men . . . ? Maybe more compensations even?' He had always envied women, just a little, himself. Their lives seemed so important, somehow. Not as disposable as those of men.

'Oh it is, Joe, we are so much more heavily programmed biologically. By comparison, for you lot procreation is a now-and-again thing, almost incidental and often unknowing, while there we are madly being programmed month after month after month for thirty-odd years, and spending our most intimate energies on motherhood. Why, even if you have only *one* child, like me, that's eighteen years or so of intimate energies – getting on for twenty, come to think of it, when you add the time trying for a baby and then the nine months. And then – it's over. You're redundant. You've done what you were put into the world to do, and that's that. And however hard you try to ignore the fact, working and seeing people and running round and kidding everyone that you were always more interested in your career than in motherhood anyway – that's still that. You could die now, and it wouldn't matter to anyone. Not really matter. You've fulfilled your function. No wonder middle-aged women take to Bridge and drink.'

He had said then, aware that his remark must sound obtuse and priggish, but needing to make it all the same:

'Well at least if you have *had* the fulfilment. Some women never achieve as much as that.'

'I know. And I know who you're talking about. I do know I'm lucky really, Joe. In fact that's part of the problem. No grand tragedy. No excuse for self-pity.'

I know who you're talking about. He had wanted very much at that moment to say more to her but had not dared to.

I do know really, I suppose, that Anna's lack of a child to bring up is central to the way she is. All that apparent independence of mind and life – yes, and body too – that precious capacity for some degree of ironic detachment: do these qualities really owe themselves to a space at the heart of things, to a biological programme (as Mary would put it) left unfulfilled? I do not want to believe so, and yet . . . I have to admit that it is important to me, in some way, that Anna is childless. She is outside those rhythms of time and season which hold Caroline and me (and apparently Mary and Tom) so firmly in thrall. Anna does not have the support of being 'Mummy' to anyone, *she* will not yearn helplessly to be a grandparent; she says she never thinks at all of such things, these days: she just is. In the end, living as they must without hostages to fortune, it is people like Anna who are the truest survivors.

There is another Anna who also just *is* in my mind, though she was not technically a survivor. There, for me, for ever. She never had children either: life gave her no chance to. Sometimes I speculate vertiginously on what her life might have been like if she had accompanied me on that June day as she so easily might have done. A good woman, says our service for the dead, 'laugheth at the days to come'. My sister Anna. The other one.

My sister Anna Buchsbaum was picked up in the street in Vienna some time in May 1942. That, by a chance testimony, I happen to know, though in all the circumstances of it I would rather not . . . She would have been just seventeen. I do not know the place or date of her ultimate destination.

Anna – Anna Morley – was born, not in Vienna but not far from it, some ten years after Anna Buchsbaum. She was born Anna Sieger. She does not remember it, or the place or anything else, because in her case her father had the foresight and fortune to remove with his entire family to London in 1938. But she is Anna Sieger all the same, inescapably, somewhere inside herself, however much she may deny it.

Anna. Two Annas, I have, forever it seems. Neither of them changes. And I really have neither of them.

Coming off the lift, to his surprise he encountered the Scottish couple from the chalet. With a look of equal surprise they greeted him affably, as two members of an élite club to a third: evidently they had not expected him to attempt such a run any more than he had expected them to. The wife was quick to tell him they had been down it once already – 'Steep, as you can see, but nothing really to worry about. Just an awkward bit with rocks after the fourth pole, isn't there, Father?'

'Blessed rockery, if you ask me.' The husband eased his efficient rucksack and settled his goggles. 'But mind you, after Aviemore we're used to the rough stuff, aren't we, Mother?'

The unconscious double meaning of this, in the man's genteel-Glasgow accent, so entertained Joe that he wished them a good second descent most warmly, and set off himself aware of a broad grin on his face.

Well, well, some people have sex and some have skiing – and some of us, lucky us, have both . . . Um, ha, carefully here, very narrow . . . Nice and steady – and swing again – there . . . Yes. Well . . . always knew the one was a metaphor for the other, like flying in dreams . . . Flying – skiing – coming – taking someone else with you . . . Ooops, nearly went a bit far there, slow down Joe . . . There, there . . . That's a better rhythm. No need to show off. No one watching you . . .

I remember once talking to an American on an aeroplane (that must have been before I was afraid of flying) – about sex. Or rather, he talked to me. Comparing women to areoplanes. He was some sort of amateur pilot, I think. Witty, *spirituel* the French call it, a bit of a fantasist I imagine, but a sort of wild realism there too. Some women, he said, are like little biplanes: you can pop them down anywhere, any patch of green field, nice and easy, provided you've got a light touch. But with some, getting them to whatever constitutes their landing is a whole high-tech performance, like getting down a Boeing – or rather, he said, warming to his theme, like *talking* a Boeing down from the control tower. Or being talked down: 'a fraction lower . . . a touch more to the left . . . Nearly! – No. Not quite. Oh dear. Check the instruments and circle round again.' We ended up rolling in our seats with inane laughter, till the air hostesses began to look worried, wondering if we were drunk. Perhaps we were, come to that. It was a business trip: there was probably free champagne.

For an unmapped stretch of time, in the blue air, he gave himself to delight. The 'little rockery' safely navigated, he swooped in sunlight over spun-glass snow, into one controlled, effective turn after another, everything working, coming together, his own bodyweight falling where it should and thus transformed into an airy nothing, at one with the radiant day.

Caroline was not enjoying herself that morning.

It was happening as it did year after year. The first day, drawing on carefully husbanded experience, she could manage nicely. But by the second day the demands of the implacable instructor had grown, and half – more than half – the class had become mysteriously more skilful and brave overnight. How did people improve so quickly? She had never known.

The instructor was talking cheerfully about taking them on a real run 'now that you all do parallels, isn't it?' The outraged teacher in Caroline (her speciality was remedial work with dyslectic children) cried out soundlessly that he was wrong. Oh, how could he not know, this genial, brutal Austrian fool, that people do not necessarily learn things all at once – that some need incessant repetition to feel competent at all?

But she set her teeth and tried to follow. The White Mouse had disappeared; no doubt she had been ruthlessly demoted to a lower class. Miss Piggy, however, was surviving, and seemed to have made friends with the agile dark boy: she would have a job keeping up with him. Oh, why this neurotic obsession with progress, why did instructors all feel they had to assure you that by the end of the week you'd be doing black runs, ha, ha, ha? Just because they got bored and restless themselves, she suspected. Why couldn't there be stay-in-one-place ski classes, consolidation classes for cautious, non-athletic people like her and Jerome, who would enjoy themselves if only they were allowed to go at their own pace . . . Jerome – where was Jerome?

She looked, and saw him at the head of the line. Evidently the instructor had called him there, he would never have gone there on his own. With his great, angular height he seemed to be stooping awkwardly. Perhaps his sticks were too short for him: either that, or he was committing the cardinal sin of watching his own feet. The instructor was shouting at him: his shoulders looked tense, his whole stance suggested controlled desperation. His anorak doesn't fit properly, she thought: to get the length he must have bought one that's too wide for him. His neck, seen rear view, seemed childish and vulnerable, as if he was still eight years old but had merely become a giant-sized eight-year-old. He hadn't changed in proportions as most boys did, as David had. David's neck, like his father's, was thick, his shoulders becoming heavy, whereas Jerome, with his mother's rangy height, seemed to have taken little or nothing from Tom but his beaky nose.

She was pierced by a sudden memory of David and Jerome as very little boys, playing with a hose in the Lovells' garden in Hertfordshire on a hot afternoon in one lost summer. With the unselfconsciousness of extreme youth they played naked, although Jennifer, older and a school child, had rejected suggestions that she might join them in this freedom and obstinately retained her knickers. David had been circumcised. (Joe had proved determined on this matter, while crossly rejecting any suggestion that his prejudice owed itself to anything but hygienic custom). Jerome was not, and Caroline, used to Joe and David, remembered now that his infantile member with its long foreskin had struck her as slightly pathetically untidy. Did he still look untidy, naked? It was a shame, she had always secretly thought, that the pristine, hairless organs of little boys and girls had to grow larger, uglier, that beastly swollen look . . .

Then she shook herself, blushing internally, and thought, Really – *really* my girl, what's the *matter* with you, thinking of Jerome in those terms? Are you going senile or something? You're disgusting and ridiculous anyway.

In any case the awful labour of skiing claimed her. The instructor was urging them up higher: a drag-lift loomed. Oh, if only one could say, No, no, I don't *want* to go up higher, I'm quite happy where I am. Impossible. She was on the conveyor belt and Jerome was at the far end of the line from her. She waited in the shuffling queue, tense and wretched. The drag, when it came, seemed a vicious one: first the bar was too low, then it jerked one suddenly upwards, clanking like some infernal machine, bumping her over humps on the worn slope so that she nearly lost her balance. Unable to seize a moment's relaxation she was borne onwards, obsessionally watching the front of her skis, terrified that one incautious move would plunge her irrevocably off into deep snow to one side or the other, leaving the class to go on without her. Lost, abandoned, skis scattered on the trackless mountain, goggles misting up, nose running . . . And I want to Go Somewhere. Oh God I want to Go –

Rooms. Anna says, when pressed, that sex is like a series of different rooms. Laughing, she says it.

Some wide open, I imagine, like this great white airy chamber in which to relax and dream. And others narrow and concentrated to the point of claustrophobia, taxing, intense: *'rocks . . . and bridges over nothing.'*

But I don't know myself. I don't really know what she means by rooms. Perhaps the simple urgencies of male sexuality exclude me from this series of rooms, this unlimited progression. I can only ask her, nagging, an over-anxious lover – and translate the answer into my own terms.

Perhaps partly because of this I now see our whole association as a chain of rooms we have been in together, as if the incidental physical surroundings that have sheltered us have also somehow been created by us. Or helped to create us.

Hotel rooms. Rooms in Frankfurt and Munich, in Paris (twice), in New York and Philadelphia and, once, for an unforgettable week, on the coast near Athens. Oh, and in Nice. And once (why? I don't remember now –) in Rouen. Rooms with large beds and tiny bathrooms, with ancient or modern flowering wallpapers and traffic grinding or sighing in the streets below. Rooms with low-wattage reading lamps and mirrors in inconvenient places. Safe rooms.

Oh, I know, I know: the banal catalogue of the classic English *affaire*, conducted in foreign cities as if these places had been conjured up solely for the purpose. '*Eros, builder of cities . . . anarchic Aphrodite.*' But we haven't been consciously romantic; it has simply happened this way, to fit in with her working life, with mine. The rooms might as well have been in Birmingham and Glasgow, Halifax, Hunstanton and Newcastle, to shelter Anna and me, Anna and me . . . But they have just happened not to be.

There is another room in the repertoire. It is not one we were in together, but she told me about it. It was in Rome, I believe. I have never been to Italy with her. I see it with unpleasant clarity. One of those grandiose Italian rooms – for I feel the hotel was an expensive one – with a high, coffered, shadowy ceiling. A statuette on the marble mantlepiece. Shallow, mirror-fronted cupboards and a great, high bed, *uno letto matrimoniale* – for a monumental marital row.

I don't know what exactly she said to Aidan in that room, what chance, infuriating, sideways, Anna-remark . . . She swears she can't remember. All I know is that he seized her and beat her. Aidan. That cold fish. Apparently it's the only time he's manifested such emotion toward her. Otherwise, she maintains, he's never said anything. Not ever. Not about me, or – anyone.

'*Beat* you,' I said, 'But do you mean – badly?'

'Oh well,' she said, looking distressed but with the faintest of giggles: evidently she was already feeling shy at having mentioned it at all, 'Not *badly* I wouldn't say. I mean, it depends what your standards are, doesn't it? I didn't end up with black eyes or anything. But my back and my bottom and my legs were covered in bruises, his hands are awfully heavy. The bruises took a couple of days really to show. When they did, he was rather embarrassed.'

'I should think he would be. I mean, I would bloody well hope so . . . What did he say then?'

'Then? Nothing.'

'Well, what did you say to him?'

'Nothing. Don't be silly, Joe. One can't *talk* about these things.'

I was shocked, deep inside myself. I still am, when I think

about it. I don't know why. I'm sure these situations are really quite commonplace, people say they are, there are all those hoary jokes about beating your wife . . . Perhaps it is simply that I have been told, in this way, something of the sexual tie that still, in spite of everything, links Aidan and Anna, and I don't like hearing it. But I prefer to think that I have always known of the undercover link between sex and violence, and am properly wary of it.

Not for nothing is death a metaphor for sexual climax. I am suspicious of the modern tendency to wish to spread a veil of reason over the whole subject: isn't this a form of neo-sentimentality and Puritanism? Silly, sub-feminist magazine tracts about the need for tender-loving-care in sexual inter-course, and penetration not being important, the sort of thing I see Caroline silently reading, on Sunday mornings – Jesus, in the last two or three years, since Caroline's cystitis or whatever in hell it is began troubling her so badly, I've exercised so much restraint and tender-loving-care on her that I feel like a bloody hermaphrodite. And still it is occasionally indicated to me that I am a selfish male, a nasty coarse brute who doesn't understand her problems or those of Women in General. Sometimes I am not surprised that violence is on the increase in our society. Oh, all right, that's a stupid, bad taste joke, but it's not entirely a joke all the same. Something dark is bound to hit back against all this sweetness and light stuff. These demands for maternity leave for men, shared domesticity and Let's-all-explore-our-femi-nine-potential-together – Sickly, obtuse female rubbish, liable only to provoke men to covert rage. Anna would never be fooled by all that. Anna knows.

Once, I don't know where, Anna said to me afterwards:

'*Oh*, I nearly got so far – right into that other room.'

'Darling . . . What other room?'

'Oh, you know, that one I've sometimes been in in dreams.' But then she smiled, so I did not know if it was a metaphor for her, or real.

'When you get there,' I said, 'you must notice what the wallpaper is like, so that you can come back and tell me.'

Perhaps her phrase so struck me because Ted – Ted Litvak – uses a phrase something like 'the other room' to mean death. No, that's not quite it: 'the other place' is what he says, I think. But that's what he means. He seems to perceive it as somewhere quite near and friendly. Not a place of horror, not the room One-oh-one by which all his family, like mine, passed. But a warm, well-lighted place. Nice wallpaper too, I expect.

Perhaps Anna's room is really inside herself. Well, I suppose it must be. What is that aphorism – I want it for my Notebook – about suffering opening places in the heart that aren't there before? I like that idea. But it doesn't necessarily work like that. Flaubert – this is in my Notebook – Flaubert wrote that he and his mistress each had a 'royal chamber' in their respective hearts, but that each had walled it up. Flaubert knew about hotel rooms in Rouen, too.

Now another unknown room awaits Anna and me. A room in Vienna. Somewhere in the Old City. Steffel nearby, the snow falling, falling into a dark chasm of courtyard beyond the double windows. What will the wallpaper be like, I wonder. How will we survive it? Another room. Then another.

Oh yes, I know it all really. In the last analysis I do not kid myself. I know that, for reasons I dare not voice to her, Anna's life and love are both end-stopped. Our love-affair (for want of another word, and it is really the only one), whatever its dynamic, is now stalemated, fixed. I know that the very thing in her life that makes her free to come to me also makes her not-mine, not anyone's. Not any more.

In my memory is another room, long and low. It is the basement, actually, of my office in Covent Garden. Three years ago I had a computer there for a bit, to play with and learn about, until I decided that it wasn't the great aid to modern life and work that it was cracked up to be, though I could see it would have some relevance to the publishing industry. Now, of course, they have become a commonplace. Anna was down there with me one evening: she had travelled from Manchester to be with me, Aidan was away somewhere. We were playing with this damn thing for hours: once started you can't leave it alone.

A few days earlier I had shown it to Ted Litvak, and he, after an initial wariness of it as 'technology', was captivated by the symbolic nature of the ideas embodied in it – the Read Only Memory seemed to him like the Jungian model of the human mind: I'd never thought of that. He particularly enjoyed a story I had heard, and repeated to him, about a man who had owned his computer for some time before he discovered by chance, pushing buttons, that its Memory contained Greek, a language he had not known it 'knew'.

(Yes, the story is meaningful for me too. In the middle years of my childhood my first language, German, sunk deep into my own memory bank, and I was innocently surprised to discover when I began to learn it again at grammar school that it was already there.)

I retailed to Anna what Ted had said. Being a linguist she liked the point about the language, but Jungian comparisons do not mean much to her: Anna likes things more graphic than that. Literally so, in this case – she began playing with the computer's Graphic Facility, which happened on this model to be much more extensive than I would ever be likely to need. (Again, you might say, like the unused capabilities of the human brain.) Computer graphics work by a collection of maddeningly inflexible symbols. One of the obvious things you can draw is a snowman – all those circles – and Anna drew one. She coloured him green, and then spent some time, with errors and erasures, giving him eyes, a nose, a mouth, a hat, ears . . . His head was very small: the hat (red) came out too large for it, I remember. Then she wanted to give him arms and legs, which turned out surprisingly difficult. She had to keep going back over her tracks, and one of the legs remained persistently deformed because she hadn't left enough room for it on the screen.

'I've had enough of him,' she said at last. 'In fact, I've quite taken against him now. Let's wipe him, and do something else.'

But we couldn't. God knows what we were doing, or

rather failing to do. That is, we could wipe him all right, but then when we pushed the next sequence of buttons that should have enabled us to proceed, instead of the word 'Enter' coming up on the blank screen that damned Green Man simply drew himself all over again. And what was worse was that it drew itself each time, though in quick motion, with exactly the hesitations, errors, erasures and repetitions with which it had been constructed in the first place. It was a perfect replication of human neurosis: a graphic illustration indeed of paranoia and obsessionalism there forever, incapable of modifying itself, refusing to go away.

At first we laughed ourselves silly. Then, as, whatever we did the horrid homunculus drew itself again and again in every detail – obese body, tiny head – it began to seem not funny at all, but nightmarish. Till at last Anna bent her head and wept bitterly, angrily, inconsolably.

After that, frantically consulting the instruction book, I think I did manage to locate our – very elementary – error and get the Green Man to disappear and not return. I still had a feeling he might be there, somewhere, in the machine's labyrinthine memory, and might come back again inadvertently, but as far as I know he never did.

In an attempt to comfort and distract her, I tried to draw a house. She did cheer up then, and blew her nose and said that she was being silly and was probably over-tired and maybe we should go and eat soon? The house was proving difficult anyway – bricks kept jumping out of the side walls and disappearing when I tried to put in the windows – so we went to eat at Les Amis du Vin, and by and by Anna smiled again and we made a joke of it all.

At lunchtime by the open-air bar there was a general fore-gathering: Joe, Tom, Mary and, unexpectedly, David and Lisette. It was crowded now, and the ten o'clock customers with their fur coats were gone as if they had never been. Joe imagined them having a lengthy set lunch in the hotel dining room, before retreating to curtained rooms. He bought beer all round, except for Lisette who did not often drink alcohol. She insisted on buying her own expensive fruit-juice and, touchingly, a second beer for him.

'But dear girl I can't drink all that, I'll be too blown up to manage up the next slope.'

'Oh, but I want you to have it – Well, share it with David, then.' She was glowing, elated by their morning together. But when David suggested that it might be fun to give that afternoon's class a miss, as it was such a fine day, and try the high run that Joe and the Lovells had done the day before, she said, a little shocked, 'Oh, we'd better go to class, David.'

'Class is only for two hours, maybe we could fit both in,' said David ruminatively.

'Remember the dark comes early. You'd be very silly to attempt anything much after three-thirty.' Joe was glad it was Tom who spoke authoritatively, not himself. Children tended to pay more attention to other people's fathers than to their own. But . . .

'Don't let the boy lead you off anywhere silly, Lisette,' he said quietly to her as they got up from the table, and was comforted by her quick smile.

Four-thirty. The light fading over the mountains like a great, cold bowl. The lower slopes, which had softened in the midday sun, becoming icy, suddenly treacherous. Joe was slogging back to the chalet, skis on shoulder, with Mary: Tom had hastened on ahead, bent on getting first turn at the hot showers. Then, coming towards them on the road, already changed into ordinary boots and trousers, was Caroline. She was shading her eyes from the sinking sun, but even before he saw her face he knew from the set of her body that she was upset about something. Oh God, what – ?

'Joe – Mary – ? Oh it *is* you, I'm glad you've come at last. Have you seen the children up that way? David and Lisette, I mean.'

The moment she said it he knew he had been waiting for it. He had been consciously worried about them and their blithe optimism when they had left the café at lunch time. During the afternoon's skiing the worry had retreated into some shut compartment of his mind and he had not disturbed it: he knew that it had been there all the time.

He and Mary looked at one another.

'I'm going back to ski over that top run,' he said, in instant decision.

'But you can't do that run *now*, idiot, it'd be dark long before you got down. Anyway, the lift-systems on that side'll be shutting – the man wouldn't even let you up.'

Caroline looked bewildered and still more distressed:

'What do you mean, the top run? Surely they can't have . . . ? I just can't think where they *are*, because their class finished an hour ago. Jerome and I saw them, up on the other side, our class was taken up that way too. I just thought you might have seen them somewhere?'

'Christ, Caro', is that all?' said Mary wearily. 'They're probably sitting in a café in the village.'

'But why should they do that, when there's tea and chocolate cake at home – at the chalet, I mean?'

Mary said with acerbic patience: 'Caroline, kids *like* sitting in cafés with new friends they may have made. They don't always want to come straight home to free cakes and Scrabble. They're not eight years old. OK, OK, if they're not back by the time night has come – and we've cased the cafés and bars – then we call out the mountain rescue service. But I really think we needn't just yet. So do cheer up! We'll all have some tea ourselves.'

This was the right way to talk to Caroline, who looked guardedly reassured. But did Mary mean what she said, Joe wondered, or was she putting it on? Had she, or had she not, registered David's idea at lunch about the top run, and Tom's warning?

'I think I'll just go back to the main lift and have a word with the chap in charge all the same,' he said, setting off before there could be any more dubious speculation.

'As you like. Caroline and I are going back to the chalet, aren't we Caro'?'

95

The man in charge of the main lift, clearly bored by Joe's anxiety, opined that there were few people up on the mountain now, and that anyway stragglers usually used the cable car to come down the last stage: it was open long after dark because of the hotel at the first lift-station.

Uncomforted, wearied by his own heavy equipment, Joe wandered back to the village. He went into several cafés, looked round for David's dark blue suit and Lisette's pink-and-light-blue one among the chattering, laughing, smoking tablefuls, but without believing they would be there. Fixed in his mind was an image of one of those perilous, lonely upper slopes, dark coming down, the young pair not following the marker poles properly, straying off-piste, Lisette becoming distressed, David trying to comfort her, rattled and anxious himself, both of them tired and inclined to do silly things, then one or the other having a nasty fall. Or, realizing they had gone hopelessly wrong, trying with an awful intrepid folly to make their own way down . . . to the edge of a dark precipice. I *knew* it, he thought, I knew it. Have known it all along.

It was almost dark in the village now, though with lights spilling onto the packed snow from the cafés and bars. The onion dome of the church at the far end was floodlit: a set for an operetta. No David, no Lisette, not in any of the places where he sought them. Wearily he turned back towards the chalet.

There, drinking tea in the lounge, were Tom, Mary, Jerome and also the Scottish couple. But not Caroline.

'She said she was just going to the other end of the village,' said Mary. 'I should leave her to it, Joe. Let's all agree not to worry till six o'clock. We'll set our watches for it. Go and have your shower, my dear, it'll revive you.'

'I should think the hot water's nearly run out,' said Tom, changed into flannel trousers, relaxed and genially unconcerned. Mary gave him an annoyed look. Joe could tell she was anxious herself.

Under the shower – Tom was right, the water was now disgustingly tepid – he replayed over and over the interchange in the café at lunch time. Had David actually announced his intention of trying that top run? Or had it just been a vague suggestion, effectively scotched by Tom?

He delayed coming down, unwilling to face further disappointment, further tension. It would soon be six o'clock.

When he finally descended it was to find Caroline, David and Lisette all in the lounge, talking and laughing with the others and demolishing the last of the cake. In an instinctual gesture, he put his arms round the two children and hugged them. Lisette looked surprised but responded warmly. David was faintly outraged –

'Now don't *you* start, Dad! Honestly – do you know what Mum did? She went and got the liftman to get us down as if we were *babies*.'

'The liftman? But I'd had a word with him already.'

'Not that lift,' explained Caroline, calm now and covertly triumphant: 'The other lift, the one that goes up the other side – I don't think you've been over there yet, have you? Jerome and I were up there this afternoon. It's one of those ones with little cars shaped like eggs – '

'The *kleine Seilbahn?*'

'Yes, I expect so. Anyway, it occurred to me that David and Lisette might have stayed up there after their lesson to have another run. So I went to the bottom of that lift and the man said it was going to close soon. He was just putting a newspaper in one of the cars. He told me – he speaks some English, that man – that when the newspaper's gone round the circuit twice with no one in the cars in between, then they stop the lift for the night. So I asked him what happened then to anyone still up on the mountain. He said you could still ski down, but I said that couldn't be a good idea, in the dark. I told him about the children and he was awfully nice and understood why I was worried and he asked what they were wearing. So I told him, and then he telephoned his mate at the top, and apparently his mate said he could see a couple dressed like that just coming down and would call to them – '

'The guy at the top thought it was a huge joke,' said

David bitterly. 'He called us over – I couldn't *think* what was up, we were fine – and then started rattling on in German and laughing at the same time. Eventually I realized he was saying "Your Mama's down below and she says you're to go down now in the lift". So we did. Huh.'

'Actually we were going to anyway,' said Lisette placatingly.

'But honestly, Mum, *honestly* – ' David turned to Caroline. 'If you fuss over us like this every time we're not home exactly when you expect us, life here's going to be *impossible*. What do you think we felt like, being ordered down as if we were twelve years old? And will you stop calling us *children* – '

'Well how else can we refer to you? There isn't another convenient word.'

'But when you say it you sound as if you still thought we wanted our noses blowing and you were determined to do it. I'm cross with you this time, Mum, I mean it.'

'Well, we were rather cross with *you*,' said Mary at once, coolly. Mothers' Trades Union. 'Never forget mountains are dangerous and night does come.'

'As if I would.'

'And I was afraid you'd done something much stupider,' said Joe sternly. 'That wild idea you had at lunch about trying the top run at the end of the day. If you don't want us to worry about you, you shouldn't throw these bloody silly suggestions into the air.'

With fear over and relief and pleasure expressed, everyone was now annoyed. Lisette looked stricken.

'We really are very sorry to have worried you all,' she murmured.

'Least said, soonest mended,' said Tom fatuously. 'Forget it.'

Lisette continued to look guilty as she and David made off upstairs, while he still exuded resentment and injured masculine pride.

'Oh dear,' said Caroline in an exhausted voice. 'Perhaps I did fuss too much. But really, they are so . . .'

'No you didn't,' said Tom with sudden resolution. 'You were quite right. Better safe than sorry. You're a good, sensible girl and we all depend on you really. Don't we, Mary? Don't we, Joe?'

Self-consciously, Joe assented.

Later, after dinner, the assorted tensions and resentments dissolved themselves into a particularly successful evening. One of the two hitherto undifferentiated men accompanying the fat woman revealed himself as an accomplished bar-room pianist, and strummed folksongs, jazz and blues in the lounge on an old upright piano with a twang like a fatal ailment somewhere in its interior. Joe kept quiet about his own, more formal ability to play, lying back in a chair enjoying the man's untaught skill. The man, whose name was Kevin, turned out to be the brother-in-law of the other, Pete, but as far as anyone could see the woman who was their linchpin treated both men with an impartial maternal tolerance. Although clad day and evening in a pink boiler suit which gave her the air of a giant baby, she did not, it was now admitted, ski herself. She liked to come 'with the lads', she said, 'for a nice rest and a breath of air. And to get on with my knitting' – shaking the enormous and elaborate Fair Isle sweater she held permanently between her capable paws.

'Goodness, how lovely, I wish I could make something like that,' said Lisette, apparently genuinely admiring.

'Don't you get a bit bored with us all going on about runs and lifts and the quality of the snow?' Joe wondered.

'Oh I don't really listen!' She laughed merrily, white teeth, flawless skin, wobbling bosom. 'Anyway, I like to see the lads enjoy themselves – and all of you, of course.'

'Pity Aidan Morley isn't here as another non-skier,' Mary murmured to Joe, 'they'd have so much in common.' Jerome, overhearing, choked into his glass of beer, and was thumped exhaustively on the back by David and Lisette, apparently assigning to him the rôle of the doormouse in the teapot.

Joe lay back in his chair, registering with a muzzy content-

99

ment a phenomenon he had noticed on ski holidays before: that in the evenings in the chalet almost anyone proved acceptable company provided that they themselves were disposed to be amiable. Mary said she liked skiing because it switched off her mind; he felt that it was, rather, some more specific trait of relentless awareness that was switched off for him by the day's taxing physical demands. Normally – at a party in London, say – the social obligation to talk to some man about cars or to some women about her children's school, drove him privately frantic with the sense of non-communication and life passing. But here tonight he did not mind what he did. He would even play poker with Kevin and Pete and anyone else who wanted to join in – Tom was busy suggesting a game – provided it was for peanuts, for *pfennigs*, rather . . .

And along with the blessed temporary release from social discrimination, there had come, he realized, a surcease from fear. Ephemeral, he guessed from hard experience, but complete. At that moment, conscious only of the warm room and the feel of the cushions beneath his tired thighs, his obscure but persistent multiform angst was simply gone. Anaesthetized or removed? As with a physical pain, he could not tell but, as also with a physical pain, its removal left only a slack, pleasant void and an optimistic hope that it might not return.

Meanwhile Caroline was in pain. Or no, not actual pain, she corrected herself: it was more of a constant discomfort, a provoking, perpetual soreness. The tensions of the day were having their revenge on her. Her cystitis was bad again.

Thank heavens, she thought wearily, no one seems to want to go Out tonight. At the best of times I've never understood all that beastly going Out to drink in some crowded bar when we can be warm and comfortable here, and tonight the very thought of putting on boots and a coat again and trudging around in the snow is hell. If I can just sit quietly, not moving at all, and making myself enjoy this nice wood fire, then perhaps after an hour or two I shall feel a bit better. Oh, how will I cope with skiing tomorrow?

No, no, I mustn't think about tomorrow, thinking about that will be Stress, and Stress makes it much worse, everyone says.

David and Lisette had in fact shown signs of wanting to go Out and take Jerome with them, perhaps to reassert their independence that had been impugned by Caroline's successful search for them. But, seeing the poker game starting, they were seduced by that instead. Lisette had not played before, and was sat down to look over David's shoulder. Tom Lovell was attired ready in his poker-playing hat, an ancient and spivvish trilby that he never failed to bring out on such occasions. To everyone's surprise the fat lady joined in, along with her consorts, and so did the husband of the Scottish couple. The wife, however, sat down beside Caroline at the fire. Caroline disliked poker, and indeed feared its playing for money . . . and all that pretending – lying, really, to call it by its proper name. She thought wistfully of the days when the children were small and the group game at this hour was Scrabble or Rummy . . . But at least they were here and hadn't gone Out.

The Scottish lady's name was, inevitably, Jean, and she seemed pleased at the chance of a chat with Caroline on her own. She, Jean, had a proposal. She had, it transpired, already spoken to Kevin and Pete and Pete's wife about it, and they said they were easy, so now she was going to ask Caroline: didn't Caroline think hey might ask those nice, obliging chalet girls if the evening meal couldn't be a bit earlier? Eight was so dreadfully late.

Caroline, scenting a classic social embarrassment, said cautiously that, yes, perhaps half past seven might suit everyone just as well. But possibly the chalet girls needed all the time they could get in order to prepare and serve a meal for fifteen people?

'Half past seven?' Jean sounded almost outraged. 'Oh, I don't think that would make much difference, would it? We were thinking about six would be nice. Or perhaps six-thirty.'

'Oh no, I don't think that would do, you know.' Caroline, divining a strong will, spoke equally firmly on her side. 'People do like to have plenty of time to relax after a day's skiing, don't they? Both my husband and Mary's usually have a nap then in fact. And after all we do get tea and all that delicious cake here between four and five; I don't think we'd really be ready to eat a full meal soon after six, would we?'

Jean sighed noisily, apparently recognizing instant defeat but making no effort to conceal her disappointment.

'I was afraid you'd say that. I told Father you would. It's you people from the south, you eat at such funny times. We always eat at six, at home, and then have a nice long evening. I like to have everything washed up and put away and tucked up for the night by seven. But perhaps it suits you all to have that late evening dinner and all that wine and then no proper cooked breakfast – '

'Well – boiled eggs for anyone who wants them. I always make a point of having one myself.'

'Yes, boiled . . .' she made 'boiled' sound as if it didn't count. 'But we're used to porridge and bacon and sausages – you know: a proper breakfast. We go to this nice guest house in Aviemore where the lady does her own baking.'

Feeling that she was perhaps tactlessly underlining a social difference but not wanting to hear about Aviemore again, and also irked by the memory of old dissension on the subject of dinner time between herself and Joe, Caroline said:

'Well we don't often eat before eight at home because my husband doesn't usually come in till well after seven.' And, once the children were past infancy, would insist that they eat with us all the same. No use my telling him that their friends mostly had children's tea still, with proper nursery things like spaghetti on toast and blancmange in the shape of a rabbit. He just said that was why English children's manners were so uncouth, because they didn't eat enough meals with adults. It was the first time he seemed really critical of me, over anything that mattered. We had a major row over it. My fault, I suppose. But – the children! I felt so hurt and sort of alone –

'Tch, seven, poor soul!' said Jean, apparently genuinely compassionate. 'Must be a long day for him?'

'Not really. He likes to stay on in the office and work quietly when the staff have gone home and there're no phone calls to bother him. That way he avoids the rush hour too. And he doesn't leave home till after half past nine in the morning. In term time I usually leave before he does.'

'Oh, you teach too?' said Jean warmly, visibly relaxing her defences. 'How nice. Yes, we're both teachers . . .'

Twenty minutes later the dispute over the meal times had been tactfully buried on a shared enthusiasm for a particular reading scheme and a comparison of the demerits of local Education Authorities, English and Scottish. Alastair (as 'Father's' name was eventually revealed to be), taught science at Arbroath Academy – 'It's a high school, you know. Very sound education.' Jean herself was a deputy head of a primary school. 'I prefer the little ones,' she said, her combative air dispersed for the moment in genuine expertise. 'They're so eager and interested in everything. Before life's got at them, you know.'

'Oh I know,' said Caroline fervently, 'some of my most persistent non-readers are wonderful children and bright as anything to talk to.' Well – it had been true of one or two. 'Er – I expect your own children are grown-up now?'

She at once sensed a tension and reticence in the other woman. But surely a couple who persistently called each other 'Mother' and 'Father' must have had at least one child?

' . . . Down's syndrome. Oh, I see. Oh – I'm so sorry.' Immediately she wished she had said something other. That wasn't the right attitude to these children, not at all, but it had just slipped out. She would much rather have said something like 'I expect he's a source of pleasure to you all, isn't he?' But she had been momentarily shocked and disconcerted because Jean had used the word 'mongol' and she herself was always very careful these days to avoid such bald terms. She had been sincerely annoyed and distressed after a recent television programme, when Joe had said it was a lot of sanctimonious hooey – that it didn't matter what you called them: cretin, idiot, mongol, Down's syndrome, intellectually disadvantaged, children with special needs – that after a decade or so *any* phrase was tainted by the reality to which it was attached, and there had to be a linguistic move into a further evasive euphemism. She still did not entirely understand what he had meant, but he had sounded so unkind, almost brutal.

Poor woman, poor Jean. No wonder she was a bit defensive about everything else. Really, life was most dreadfully unfair. When you thought about it, it was hardly bearable.

'People say that Down's syndrome children are often very affectionate – and musical?' she hazarded, wanting it to be true.

'People say a lot of things,' said the other woman, with the restraint born of individual experience. 'What they forget is that these children don't stay children all their lives – except in one sense. Jimmy's a great strong lad now, and clumsy with it, and it's no joke having one of those around with an IQ below forty.'

'I can imagine,' Caroline murmured, chastened.

'Well – I say "around" but just this last year we've got a permanent place for him, boarding. Weekly boarding, that is: we normally have him home every weekend. To be frank, it's been a great relief to both of us. We're neither of us getting any younger. We were wearing ourselves out, and sometimes you ask yourself, What's the point of it all? You really do . . . Where he is now, he can stay till he's twenty-eight. After that – ' She made the very small, hopeless gesture of one faced with an insuperable problem it is no use contemplating.

'We've got some friends with a badly handicapped child.'

'Oh yes?' The other woman was clearly all too used to this response, and her tone was hardly encouraging, but Caroline, once embarked on this forbidden territory, found herself continuing:

'Yes. Microcephalic, poor little thing. You know – a tiny head that never grows bigger. He was born – oh, years ago now. A lot later than our two, but even so he must be twelve or thirteen now. He's been in a Home almost since birth. In fact I've never seen him. I must admit, it seems rather awful to me that they just put him right away.'

'Probably the best thing they could have done,' said Jean unexpectedly and harshly. 'I've seen microcephalics, there's some in the place Jimmy's in now. At least you know where you are with them – nowhere. They stay like babies in nappies. With mongols, there's always the chance they may turn out quite high grade. So people string you along for years – doctors and psychologists and so on. They mean well, of course. But.'

And Caroline, who had been half looking forward to a safe, consoling discussion, out of Joe's hearing, on the heartlessness of parents such as Aidan and Anna Morley, was discountenanced and fell silent.

– I shall never understand why Joe regards it as such a deadly secret, as if having a handicapped baby was something to be *ashamed* of. He said I should never mention it to Anna or Aidan themselves, and gets somehow annoyed if I refer to their child even to him. It's ridiculous. We're not living in the Middle Ages. Can't we be civilized about these things? I mean, several people besides ourselves must *know* of the child's existence. Other people who knew the Morleys when it was born – the Lovells must know. But when I mentioned it once to Mary I got the impression that she thought the baby had died quite soon after birth, and I didn't quite like . . . She didn't want to talk about it, either, I could tell. I was surprised: a super-intelligent women like her, and so ready to blab on about all sorts of other things.

After that, I checked with Joe because I wondered if the boy *had* died, and I thought he would probably know, I mean he's always been so matey with Anna and Aidan, I can't quite think why, I suppose it's just more of the Oxbridge Mafia. I was going to be jolly cross with him, if it *had* died and he hadn't even told me. I mean, I am his wife. But apparently it was – is – still alive.

I told Joe then that I was quite sorry for Anna really. And he said grumpily, not understanding, Well of course you are: we're all sorry for a couple whose only child is born a hopeless vegetable. It's a tragedy: there's no other word to use. And I said, No, I didn't mean that, I meant that I was quite sorry for anyone who'd been able to just to push their handicapped child out of sight and carry on airily with life as if the whole experience had meant nothing to her.

I'm still not sorry I said it. I still think it's true. But Joe was frightfully angry with me. It was years ago, but I still think of it sometimes when I wake in the night. He needn't have been so horrible. He said that I understood nothing and that that was the basis of my enormous smugness. Yes, he said that. Smug. *Me*. Much he knows, conceited, selfish pig. Joe Beech, with his heart on his sleeve, just revelling in being loved by everyone –

Oh I know it was perhaps unfair of me to say it. After all, I don't really know Anna, not like Joe seems to. And, unfair or not, it was stupid of me anyway, as he thinks she's so marvellous. I can't think quite why he thinks that, particularly as we hardly ever see the Morleys these days. Oh, perhaps that is why . . . Or perhaps – ?

No. *No*, I won't think like that. No, I won't even let it cross my mind. That's middle-of-the-night stuff, when you think everyone is secretly plotting against you, black misery, like being homesick at boarding school and not letting on to anyone ever, ever, ever, because they would just give you a worse time. I won't let that slime-trail of fear get at me, I *won't* – Remember Stress. Breath. Relax . . .

But I must admit I'm relieved Anna hasn't come on this holiday, anyway. I just don't think she'd have fitted in. Not these days.

'I say – do we have a plastic dustbin lid?' The Non-scorer, bescarfed and blotchily red in the face, had materialized in the warm room, bringing with him a blast of the icy end-of-the-year night. In the last two days the weather had turned reassuringly colder. Rude shouts of 'Shut that door!' arose from the poker party, which was becoming riotous. Cowed, he retreated, shut it, and then came back to stand in the middle of the carpet to repeat his demand in his loud, flat Midland accent. Joe, feeling sorry for this perpetual wanderer between two chalets – eating and sleeping at one while socially committed to the other – said:

'What did you want it for?'

'I know,' said Mary, sitting wreathed in cigarette smoke, 'It's *poubelling*, isn't it. Sooner you than me on a night like this!'

'*Poubelling?* I don't know.' The young man looked flustered but vaguely defiant. 'The chaps next door just asked me to come and see if there were any more lids here. They're using them to slide down the slope across the road.' Indeed, while the door had been open, muffled shouts and whoops had penetrated the insulated room.

'Across the road!' said Scottish Jean censoriously. 'It's not made up as a piste. You'll all get soaked.'

'You do realize, don't you,' said Tom Lovell, imitating her tone deadpan, 'That it's damn dangerous.'

The boy wavered, all eyes on him.

'Oh-o – is it really?'

'Oh most frightfully,' said Jerome, taking his cue from his father. 'We knew a fellow the other year who did it – didn't we David? – and, well, I don't like to go into sordid details, but he was never the same after.'

'Oh Jerome, that *can't* be quite true – ' Lisette began, but was stopped by a face from David and lapsed into suppressed giggles.

'I', said Tom ponderously, 'I myself will take it upon myself to find you a suitable bin lid – since I should think our doughty chalet girls are all out by now on the town if they know what's good for them. But as long as you understand I take no responsibility for what might happen.'

'Of course, I quite understand,' said the Non-Scorer earnestly, adding as an afterthought: 'Ta very much.'

The moment the door to the kitchen regions had closed on Tom and the young man there was an explosion of laughter.

'What brutes we are!' said Mary cheerfully.

'Well as long as Tom finds him his damn lid,' said Joe. 'Then we'll all be happy.'

A few minutes later they reappeared, Tom ushering the Non-Scorer straight out through the front door with many elaborate reassurances and hopes of his safe return.

'But Tom, that wasn't a dustbin lid he had in his hands,' said Caroline as soon as the door had banged shut.

'No, you're quite right, it wasn't.'

'It was a plastic bag,' said Mary. 'Tom, you *are* a brute! Making the poor little bugger lose face with his mates like that.'

'Serve him right for being such an idiot,' said Tom cheerfully, sitting down at the card table again with a great jolt.

'He won't be able to toboggan on a bag, will he?' said Lisette.

'Should hardly think so!'

'So he *will* be quite safe,' said Kevin and Pete's fat lady, and everyone began to laugh helplessly again.

Skiing makes everyone so *silly*, thought Caroline, sitting on by the fire. And I've never been any good at being silly. When we were all younger, I used to try to pretend to enjoy things as much as they did, all their in-jokes . . . But I think I'm too old now. Although Joe and Tom seem to get sillier the older they get, and all the rest egging them on – how can they? That wretched boy with his acne. Oh maybe it's just that I'm so chronically sore. It does take the fun out of things, being sore. And Joe simply doesn't seem to understand. He doesn't mean to be unkind, I daresay. He isn't really an unkind man, I do know that. But he doesn't understand.

Late that night in bed he turned to her. Tired and content from the evening they had spent, he essayed a few moves. But, sensing that she was only lying there suffering it, nascent desire died in him and he contended himself with patting her stomach inconclusively.

'I'm sorry. It's bad again . . .' Her voice was wretched.

'Never mind, it doesn't matter,' he said – and then knew that that wasn't really a comforting thing to say, not what she would want to hear, but could not make any further or different effort tonight.

Suddenly out of the dark she said:

'You do think I did right – don't you? Going to look for the children, I mean.'

'Yes,' he said gently, unable to contradict on account of his own black fantasies, even though he would not divulge these to her – 'Yes, I think you did right.'

They lay in silence for some time. She, on her side, thought he might have gone to sleep, till he said:

'But you can't hold them, you know. *We* can't hold them. They are right, they aren't children any more: you can't always keep tabs on them. They are going away to lead their own lives – have more or less gone already. It's really only by chance that they're with us this week at all. They might easily have made other arrangements. Next year maybe they will.'

'I know that,' she said tonelessly. He wondered if she really did.

Presently, across the great, lonely space that was between them, he took her hand in his. Joined at least in their mutual loss, they drifted into sleep. But some time in the night, in spite of his physical tiredness, he was abruptly jerked from sleep, chaotic dreams wheeling backwards and then snapping off like a spool of film breaking, leaving him awake, alone, twitching faintly in the dark.

Fear had returned.

5

'Mr Beech! Mr Beech!'

Joe, having lain awake for what seemed a large part of the night, had fallen into a heavy sleep near dawn. Struggling out of it, through layers of dream and confusion, he realized that the girl knocking insistently on the door was calling him to the telephone.

'I'm coming – '

Tense, mind already racing – *Who? What? What mishap?* – he searched ineffectively for his dressing gown and then remembered he had not brought it. He pulled his ski anorak over his pyjamas and went downstairs in his bare feet. No one else was up yet, but there was a Continental early morning smell of coffee which took him back fugitively, as if he were continuing his dreams, to another place and time. Light gleamed white through the windows. Under the skis in the hallway rack small puddles of melted snow had gathered. He shivered as he picked up the phone.

'Joseph? It's Aidan. Aidan Morley.'

'Aidan – Christ. Is – that is, is everything all right?' He passed a hand over his sleep-sodden face, trying to summon resources to deal with whatever blow was to come.

'Well, in a manner of speaking. My flu is on the wane, if that's what you mean.'

'Oh – Oh, I'm glad.'

Damn, I should have asked. I'd forgotten his sodding flu. Maybe I didn't believe in it anyway.

'Did I wake you?' said Aidan, not apologetically but, Joe thought, accusingly. 'It's seven o'clock here. I believe you're one hour ahead of us, and I was afraid I might miss you if I rang later.'

'Yes. Quite right.' Joe leant back against the wall, feeling in his pocket for a handkerchief and wishing that his heart, which he now realized had begun thumping in his chest at the sound of Aidan's voice, would calm down. (A heart

110

attack! Now *there* was a new and fruitful source for worry.)
Nothing dreadful could have happened to Anna – could it?
– if Aidan were wittering on about his own flu and the time
in England. Not, however, that 'wittering' appropriately
described Aidan's customary remote, subliminally angry
telephone manner.

'I have tried,' said Aidan, in the same measured tone, 'to
get Anna to come out and join you all for the last three days.
She says it's not worth it. I think that's ridiculous, as she
had to go to this workshop in Zurich in any case.'

'Workshop in Zurich?' said Joe at random. 'I don't think
I know about that.'

'A Modern Language function she's got on early in the
New Year.'

Impatiently. 'I thought she would have mentioned it to
you – anyway, she'll be going to that, and as my temperature's gone down now and I'm really perfectly all right apart
from a stinking cold and cough, there's no earthly reason
why she shouldn't fly out to Zurich today. But she says she
won't.' He paused, and the pause came just at the point
where Joe, making his own bewildered calculations, realized
that Anna must have used the coming academic workshop
as her pretext, genuine or otherwise, for being in Europe in
the New Year.

'I just thought I'd ring you myself,' said Aidan stiffly, 'so
that you know it's not *my* doing she hasn't come.'

'Very thoughtful of you, Aidan.' Christ. What do I mean?

Half a minute later Aidan had rung off. Joe stood there a
long moment, cradling the receiver in his hands, before he
replaced it.

A fine start to the day. That could not – could it? – have
been Anna herself indicating in code through Aidan that she
was not after all going to join him?

Oh don't be a fool. Anna would ring herself, if that were
the case. And anyway, if there were a message in code there
it was more the opposite: almost as if Aidan were saying,
'It's OK. She's coming eventually.'

Relinquishing this line of speculation as unfruitful and

unnerving, Joe made his way upstairs again. On the landing he encountered his son, rumpled, halfclad.

'Hallo, Dad,' said David self-consciously, and then, as to defend himself in apparent bravado, 'And where are *you* coming from at this hour? Or shouldn't I ask?'

'You,' said Joe, annoyed and not amused, 'are a fine one to talk.'

'What do you mean?' David, realizing his man-to-man joke had misfired, feigned injured innocence. 'I've been to have a pee, if you really want to know. And now I'm going back to our room. OK?'

On an angry impulse, Joe said:

'I don't blame Lisette. She's our guest, more or less; obviously she takes her cue from you. But I think it's a bit mean of *you* to have left Jerome to sleep with the Non-Scorer.'

'Huh, sleep with the Non-Scorer, that's all *you* know, Dad!' David's voice rose with righteous indignation. 'What you *don't* know, because you lot went to bed before it happened, is that late last night that bloody Non-Scorer came in pissed as a newt and started blundering around trying different doors. I suppose he was getting desperate, what with No Score and that plastic bag business, and was hoping for a spare chalet girl – or the White Mouse. Jerome told him not to be such an ass and to go to bed, and then the Non-Scorer started ranting on in their room. So we told Jerome to leave him to it and move his mattress into our room. And that's how we've been all night: me in one single bed, Lisette in the other, and Jerome on the floor between us threshing around in his usual way.'

'I see. Poor Jerome.'

' – So I hope you're satisfied that I'm doing my duty by Jerome. Don't you come priggish with me, Dad. You say I'm a fine one to talk, but I might point out that Lisette is my girlfriend, official and above board, and neither of us has anyone else. If anyone's a fine one to talk it's *you*. Isn't it?'

In the silence that followed this remark, Joe distractedly registered that David's voice had become steadily louder as he spoke and that they were standing at one end of a corridor of bedroom doors.

'For God's sake keep your voice down. You'll wake the whole chalet.'

'Everyone'll be getting up soon anyway, but that isn't really what you're afraid of, is it? . . . Look, Dad, *I* don't care what you do when you're away from home. It isn't my business. But just realize that not everyone is fooled. Mum may be – I don't know, and I'm not going to talk to her about it, so don't start wetting yourself. But I'm not, and nor is Jenn and nor, I have the impression, are the Lovells. So – I've been wanting to say this – just watch yourself, Dad. That's all.'

And, victorious, he returned smartly to his room.

Left alone on the landing in the snow-bright early morning light, Joe felt as intimidated as if his son had physically assaulted him.

How the hell did the boy know? He and Anna had always been so careful . . .

Oh, it was probably just intuition and a wild guess that had happened to find its mark. David was like him in many respects, there had always been a lot of understanding and sympathy between them as well as rivalry. And now that David himself was a man . . .

Very likely he had no idea, in fact, whom it was that his father secretly met. Trying to comfort himself with this idea, Joe began to mount the second flight of stairs, back to Caroline. But he still felt shaken and wretched. David's words. And, before that, Aidan's call . . . It was as if that Other room of which Anna had spoken, that ultimate room that was apparently inside both of them, had been violated. The secret place, crudely exposed.

How will we ever find it now?

Just as the assembled party were finishing breakfast a telegram arrived and was handed to Joe.

'Not another bulletin on Aidan's flu?' said Mary. 'This is getting quite exciting!'

113

But Joe saw Caroline's face looking stricken and felt her thinking – Jenn? – The house? He opened it quickly.

It was from Ted Litvak's daughter Naomi. Ted had died suddenly, of a heart attack, the previous day. The funeral was on Sunday. Would Joe please ring Naomi?

Among the general murmur of concern and sympathy that went round the table, Joe was aware of sighs of relief, a slackening of the instant tension that telegrams, ever since 1914, have engendered. (No wonder Britain had abolished internal telegrams.) The tacit agreement is that old men are allowed to die, their deaths do not much frighten us. Ted was only in his sixties, but he had long been rotund, grey-haired, balding. He may have died unexpectedly but full of honour, replete with disciples and friends, famed for placidity, his essential work long accomplished . . . let us all relax, and have another cup of coffee.

But – oh Ted. Joe sat there in front of his unfinished bread roll, and grieved inexpressibly for the only father his adult years had known.

'What a morning,' said Tom, who obviously resented the way outside messages were impinging on the sealed snowstorm-ball world of the skiing holiday. 'Better go and phone the daughter now, hadn't you old boy, and get it over?'

'Yes. I will.' But Joe went on sitting there. He was giving himself up briefly to the weak fantasy that Ted was not really dead after all, that the telegram was a mistake. Once he had spoken to Naomi all such pretence would be over.

'Yes, you'd better ring,' said Caroline fussily. 'Do you think she will want you back for the funeral? I wonder where it will be.'

'I don't know.' Stop asking me these things. I'm not ready to think about them yet.

To show he was not going to be pushed by anyone, he sat there several more minutes before getting to his feet.

The funeral was to be at a Jewish cemetery to the north of London, and yes, Naomi, loquacious with grief and with

114

the effort to surmount it, was hoping very much that he would be able to be there.

'I was really hoping, Joe, that you'd do the eulogy. Well, to be honest, I thought first of Martin and Tonia Ayres, as they're really Daddy's oldest friends of all in London, but he's not Jewish and of course it has to be a male Jew . . . *Could* you do it, Joe?'

'My dear . . . Of course I would say yes, but – well, for one thing, Naomi, I've hardly set foot in a synagogue since I was a small child. I never had a *barmitzvah*, you see. I'm not even sure if I count.'

Lies, Joe, lies. Judaism is not just a cult. A Jew is a Jew forever, you know that perfectly well, however far his life or his scepticism carry him into alien paths. He felt that Naomi, across the mountains and valleys of Europe, must know this and be instantly discounting his specious excuses. Ashamed of them already, he hastened to offer something nearer the truth:

'Also – on Sunday, did you say? I'm dreadfully afraid there is a further problem of organization here.'

'When I rang your house your cleaning lady said you would be back on Sunday. She didn't know what time of day, but the funeral isn't till the afternoon. I did hope . . .' Terrier Naomi, only daughter of an impractical widower. Blast the poor woman, she must surely realize that he was most unlikely to get all the way from the remote mountains of the Tyrol to a cemetery in a distant London suburb within the confines of a short winter day? But of course why should she? She had something larger to think about. And in any case, as it happened, Sunday's timetable was irrelevant.

'Unfortunately it's only Caroline and the kids who are coming back then. I'm due to stay abroad till the end of the week – no, no, not here, business in Vienna. Naomi, I *am* sorry . . .'

'It doesn't matter,' she said, in a small, disappointed voice.

'If it were only a matter of getting home from here, I'd try to get a place on a flight a day early,' he said, stricken with guilt, meaning it.

115

'Oh goodness, why should you? It'd probably cost – oh no, it would be ridiculous.'

'It isn't that. It's that I've got – that is, I've got appointments in Vienna already lined up for Monday.' That at least was true, if only part of the truth. 'Naomi, you do understand, don't you?'

'Of course I do. And so would Daddy. Of course you can't go flying backwards and forwards all over the place. He'd be awfully cross if I tried to make you, on his account.' He could hear she was near to tears. 'But oh Joe! I would have liked you to be at the funeral.'

In an agonized need to shut her up, he said, 'Look, Naomi, look – this is just the funeral. A family-and-close-friends affair?' He remembered that Ted had had no family bar Naomi, and hurried on – 'But later there'll be a memorial service – has to be, an eminent man like that: well look, let me organize that for you, mmm? Not in a hurry over New Year when people are away, but some nice convenient time like the middle of February. OK?'

'Will you really do that, Joe?' He could feel her glow down the phone with surprised pleasure. Naomi was very unassuming; it probably had not even occurred to her that a memorial service would be appropriate.

'I promise,' he said.

After that, he ended the conversation as soon as he decently could.

Unfaithful. Not only an unfaithful husband but also an unfaithful friend. And, worst, in this case something close to an unfaithful son as well. No, Ted, so mild and fair, would not think so: he would not, as his daughter says, think I should go flying back and forth across Europe just to stand by the broken earth of his grave, to pronounce words and to shovel London clay onto his loved, discarded body. But *I* think I should.

Shame and guilt. Guilt and shame. And pity, too, for Naomi, and guilt therefore as well towards her. And therefore anger. This, the heart's hardening, my son, is where

116

unfaithfulness leads you: you know that, you have been warned, it is written already in your damned Notebook, the Book of Damnation –

> There was a man of double deed
> Sowed his garden full of seed;
> When the seed began to grow
> 'Twas like a garden full of snow . . .

Snow in my heart instead of flowers, nothing growing there. No children will ever germinate from my seed in the secret garden I have with Anna. Just mounds of white snow like fantasy blossom, so beautiful, but smothering and blocking everything else . . . And snow lying too between me and Caroline, Caroline and me, in a great white expanse, a hinterland unswept for skiers, a frozen mountain.

Caroline remarked once, ostensibly joking but with some asperity, that Naomi Litvak has been in love with me for years. I was surprised when she said it, as such remarks aren't much in her line, and also because, though it had not occurred to me before, I realized that it was true. I won't be made responsible for that as well; women do fall in love with me sometimes even when I haven't slept with them: secretaries, unhappy academics who are writing books for me. I cannot feel guilty about everyone – but now I have failed Naomi in the one area where she does have some solid claim on me, some right to expect . . . I have let her down, and thus let Ted down. Damn. Oh *damn*.

Naomi is a social worker, a short, broad-hipped girl with Ted's face that does not sit well on a woman; fine dark eyes, badly dressed, given to hopeless causes and to optimistic environmental explanations of human behaviour. Has inherited all of Ted's gentleness and sympathy but fewer of his brains – a disappointment to him, not because of that but because she has not married. She should have been a wife to some dependent man and capable mother to his children, not yearning over the ungrateful and exploitative derelicts of Islington.

Perhaps *I* should have married Naomi. Then Ted really would have become in some sense my father, and, with Naomi, I would have given him his grandchildren. It might have been more logical than the marriage I did make; a return, via the tortuous dislocations of exile, to the fold from which I originally came.

Oh don't be so ridiculous. If Caroline infuriates you with her socially-responsible-JP-and-making-heavy-weather-of-it airs, how much more so would Naomi have done with her preoccupation with the underdog and her facile, Greenham Common Armageddonism? Just imagine how she would annexe your personal fears to her own distorted belief system. She would madden you, and you would be awful to her. Don't add sentimentality, of all things, to your other sins.

When they were upstairs preparing for the day ahead, Caroline said:

'I think you ought to go to Ted's funeral. He cared a lot for you.'

'I know that, dammit.' He felt tears come prickling behind his lids as she voiced the fact and so made it inescapably true. 'And I cared for him – oh, more than I can say.' And more than you can realize, Caroline. 'But I *can't go* and that's that.'

'Well – you *could* – '

'You know what I mean.'

Does she? I have a horrible feeling she may.

But if Caroline did suspect the true source of his decision, when she spoke again after a prolonged and disapproving pause it was to make quite another accusation.

'I think,' she said, in her best detached but 'concerned' manner, 'that you are trying not to face the fact that Ted is dead.'

'Since however he is dead that would seem neither here nor there.' Joe spoke as coldly and discouragingly as he could, willing her to shut up, but it was apparently a matter of principle with her to continue.

'You want to avoid the funeral because his death makes

118

you feel guilty . . . Death *does* make people feel guilty, you
know.'

Tension that had been building up since he was woken by
Aidan's call seethed inside him.

'I don't not want to go to the funeral because I feel guilty,
for Christ's sake. It's the other way round.'

Obstinately she continued:

'Perhaps you think, at some level, that Ted dying suddenly
like that, while you're away, is your fault.'

The tension rose upwards like milk and boiled over.

'Of all the bloody stupid things to say. Don't you try
your phony, do-gooding, amateur Freudianism on me,
Caroline. And don't you try to contaminate Ted with it
either. As you say, I cared for Ted, so you keep your hands
off him and me. You can't own what Ted and I had, whatever smug, know-all airs you put on, so don't try to.'

Caroline's knuckles on the straps of her ski boots were
white. 'I'm not trying – '

'Yes you are! You just can't face that there are things you
don't know and don't understand and had better leave alone.
It's not only you, it's the same for everyone – but *you* won't
accept it. You have to go around patronizing everyone by
understanding them, don't you? And being *sorry* for them,
God dammit, because they haven't achieved your half-baked
insights. Insights, indeed! As if *you* had any insights into
people like Anna and Aidan – or into Tom and Mary, come
to that – *or* into that frightful woman you sit on the Bench
with and who you're so sorry for because her husband
deserted her – '

'Well he did desert her – ' Frantically.

'I know that! And I expect he's a coarse, selfish oaf – he
certainly looked like it, the one time I set eyes on him. But
the point is, *you* can't accept that he's just a straightforward
out-for-number-oner, can you? You swallowed a lot of guff
from his wife about his state of mind and his relationship
with his mother, and went round *yourself*, you interfering
cow, to try to persuade him to have psychotherapy and be
"cured". As if one can be *cured* of wanting to leave one's

119

wife! It isn't an ailment. It isn't, contrary to what you like to think, a neurosis. It may be brutal, but also perfectly logical. And no wonder he ran off even harder when his wife co-opted you on her side. Jesus Christ, Caroline: you may be able to know best for those wretched, dim little kids you teach – sorry, "underachievers" – and you may know best on the Bench (though I wouldn't be too sure about that) – but *just don't try it on with your equals*. And, more than anything, don't try it on with me.'

All the way to the lift-station on his own Joe violently justified himself.

Caroline had made no reply to his diatribe. If not quite unprecedented, it was at any rate unprecedentedly long, and probably the unkindest thing he had ever said to anyone. For once, she had been silenced, and had simply turned away from him. But, leaving the room with his temper still flaring, Joe had caught a sideways view of her stricken face, and in a moment of – no, not regret, but remorse – had crossed the room and laid a craven hand on her shoulder before beating as hasty a retreat down the stairs as his ski boots allowed.

No, not regret. Rather, the exhilarating feeling of having, for once, behaved with naked brutality, unrestrained by prudence or decency. *'Wanting to leave one's wife is not an ailment, Caroline. It isn't a neurosis . . . It may be perfectly logical . . .'* Let her be told that! It's time she faced it –

A quieter voice hinted in his conscience that almost any shoddy act or base desire can be clothed in rationality: that the first impulse of the traitor is to draw a personal bill of indictment against those he is preparing to betray. The cad's department, this. Fabricated accusations, pre-processed excuses. The 'reasons' for perfidy put on display for public view. The facile wisdom that if you quarrel you'd be better apart leading to assiduously manufactured quarrels. *The foul rag and bone shop of the heart . . .*

But, in his blinding, accumulated irritation, he closed his ears to the voice. In his outburst his resentment had not spent itself, rather it seemed to have been let out of its cage like a dangerous animal and was now ranging free. He was sweating as he strode along, even though the morning was cold and the day's exertions before him.

In such times – for there had been others before now – the dream of running away to a brand new life would once more assert itself, temporarily as heady and all-consuming as it had been five years ago, as seductive in its outrageous simplicity. In such moments he knew that men who leave their wives, women who leave their children, people who abandon home and career and reputation to go precipitously down another path, do so not in spite of the daunting ruthlessness and folly of such an act but *because* of it. Beyond a certain point destructiveness is its own justification. Uncomfortable, small-scale personal realities are blotted out by the grand archetype, as you make your heroic, irretrievable, once-only bid for freedom, for escape – from what, exactly, no longer matters. The past is not merely abandoned but burnt, dramatically, behind you.

He was talking in his mind, now, to an imaginary listener: Ted Litvak. I had an Uncle Sigi who made such an escape, he told Ted, at once regretting that he had never told him in life, because Ted was interested in this sort of story . . . An uncle by marriage, actually – and therefore, perhaps, less contaminated with the family reasonableness and caution than were the rest of the tribe. But that is different (isn't it?) because he knew what he was escaping from. 1939. At about the same time that I was seen off on my train at the Westbahnhof, Onkel Sigi left his wife, my mother's sister, and got away to America on some sort of business permit. Of course it wasn't *called* leaving his wife: the theory – as I learnt long afterwards from my distant American cousins – was that, once he was safe with them, he would set about getting his wife and the rest of the family out. And probably he did seriously intend to, but I suspect that he also knew in his heart that it would not work – that they would not drop everything and come, would not relinquish home, money, identity, country, other people, every possession, because they simply would not comprehend that such a desperate act was really the only one left to them. They lacked imagination, I suppose, lacked too the necessary ruthlessness. Kind and reasonable themselves, incapable of true evil, they could not quite bring themselves to face the evil that confronted them even when it was almost upon them. Yes, yes, they knew things were very grave, and if war was coming anyway the business would have to be abandoned, they would all be ruined. But surely in that case they must try to save what they could? Would the American cousins pay for some of the furniture to be shipped? They would eventually be paid back in full – A boat was due to leave Trieste for New York on July 10th . . . No, that one was now almost full, and there was valuable stuff from the Turkenschanzplatz house also, not to mention Aunt Sophia and all her family . . . Another boat was due to leave on August 5th for Baltimore . . . for Boston . . . No, for San Francisco, going all the way round the world the other way, but perhaps that did not matter, it was all America, wasn't it? September 3rd, that ship was due to sail, from Marseilles . . . Would the American cousins ask . . . would they guarantee . . . ? Contorted, cross-purposes telegrams flew back and forth across the Atlantic. The cousins themselves, comfortable in Philadelphia, became caught up in the fantasy that there might still be time to arrange this, to think of that, to save the other . . . Finally, at the end of August, in the week the German army marched into Poland, Uncle Sigi sent his wife a cable – *Komm sofort. Notfalls alleine* – 'Imperative you come now, alone if necessary'. She did not come, and perhaps he had known she wouldn't. She and my mother had always been very close, and my father was just hoping, arranging . . . On September 2nd France declared war on Germany: no boat sailed from Marseilles on the 3rd or, if it did, no one from central Europe was on it. The cousins sent off several more telegrams but from the clan in Vienna a great silence fell. And remained.

All this I heard many years later, in a suburban house in Pennsylvania. I was making a brief visit to my unknown, genial, alien semi-relatives – cousins really only by courtesy – while on a publishing trip to New York. They were old then, I believe they are both dead now. In any case, by the time I came to America my Uncle Sigi, our one family link, the escaper, the one who faced what was happening and dared leave, the survivor, was no longer there to welcome me.

The survivor. I suspect he was that by nature, actually, long before the violence of fate and his own acumen turned this general personality trait into a specific and terrible fact. Out of the shadowy recesses of my early childhood he appears to me now, not in any recognizable detail but as a figure of some charm and nonchalance, the sort of indulged brother who is habitually late when invited to lunch, the sort of uncle a little boy may readily regard as his official 'favourite'. He was, or seemed, younger than all my other aunts and uncles: perhaps even then I, another youngest, vaguely identified with him.

In my quite other, English, later childhood, during the war and the years of rationing that followed it, food parcels for me from Uncle Sigi arrived from America at long intervals. At least, I know that each time one came I, growing and changing, had forgotten I even had a Uncle Sigi, and had to be reminded about him over again. Tins of ham and sardines, chocolate, packets of dried fruits that my foster mother, with expressions of pleasure, made into heavy cakes. And, just once, a short letter, partly in German, partly in faulty English, both of which embarrassed me. I had to take it to a master at school to get it read completely. It did not say much beyond assurances of his own wellbeing, currently with a fur-trading company in Seattle, hopes for mine, exhortations to become a good scholar and promises that he would write at greater length 'soon'. Not a word about all his, and my, lost family, our lost world. And he never did write again.

For both these reasons my foster parents, and my teacher, were sorry for me. They did not say so, but I was old enough by then to tell that they thought my one surviving relative, even if only an uncle by marriage, might have tried to keep in touch with me. But I did not blame him. I admired, and thought I understood. I was old enough as well to feel I had some inkling of what that great leap out of the closing prison of central Europe and into the fresh, primeval darkness of another world, must have meant to him. Of course the old world had to die, not just literally and horribly, but die for *him*, country, wife, relatives, friends, in order that he might live elsewhere. Talk about the New Life dream: my Uncle Sigi, an exception to most men, actually made it come true.

I was irritated by the grown-ups' tactful solicitude for me, and thought it quite natural that my Uncle Sigi did not want to have much to do with me now, any more than I did with him. I wished him well, with his fractured American-English and furs from the Yukon on the far side of the world, but I was now an English schoolboy.

It was a very long time, decades indeed, before I began to see matters differently – began to lose, you might say, my own survivor's ruthlessness – and by that time Uncle Sigi, Onkel Sigi . . .

He found himself at the top of the main cabin lift, clattering down the iron stairs with the throng who would then disperse in all directions. So deep and sudden had been his plunge into memory on leaving Caroline that he had followed the customary route automatically without making any conscious choice. He had aimed simply at regaining the clean, anaesthetic heights and solitudes on his own. He wanted no one. For the moment they could all do without him.

But this morning this escape, too, was subtly denied to him, for the sparkling morning whiteness that he had seen early from the windows and had expected on the mountain was now veiled. There was whiteness all right, all around, but a heavy, yellowish whiteness from the sky itself, which was not arched above the peaks but lying low upon them. The contours of the landscape, instead of standing out in brilliant relief, were dulled, white on white, like a picture that is insufficiently lit, the perspective flattened. The furthest, highest mountain range was invisible, as if wiped out by a giant erasure.

'Looks like it may be snowing up there,' someone said in German near Joe as he stood fitting on his skis by the hotel terrace.

He did not heed the voice. He was intent on getting up higher and again higher, away from other people. Away.

A chair lift a couple of hundred yards to the left led up, according to his pocket map, to a plateau, a long but shallow drag-lift, and from there a circuitous but quite easy run down a chain of valleys to St Wilhelm, the next village. He set off, and soon swung out alone in his chair into the blessed, dreamlike silence. The thought came into his mind, as it had before, 'I hope that dying will be like this' – and then he wondered what it had been like for Ted: how sudden, how frightening or painful? – and sent out a passionate wish into the icy air that his old friend's last minutes had not been too terrible, but like this: a violent shift, a roaring of the human machinery in his ears, then a strangeness, a detachment, an airborne journey into a bright nothing as the world fell away below him.

At the top of the lift it was very cold. As he slid off his seat and skied down the slope to the plateau, a flurry of miniature snowflakes stung his cheek. Few people were about.

He located the drag-lift. It was stationary as he reached it, and unattended: only when he had shuffled his skis into line and approached the bar did the winding gear rattle into life. A notice said, 'Nur für erfahrene Schifahrer'. Well, all right.

It was a long, bumpy ride that, disconcertingly, took him down slopes a couple of times as well as up them, past acres of rough whiteness unswept by any piste: no wonder they warned inexperienced skiers off this run. It was snowing now, not much but indisputably, a fine white sandpaper blowing across his goggles, scraping his cheeks and lips. He realized that he had left the hotel that morning in too much of a hurry to remember his stick of lip salve. Too bad.

In another mood he would have been wary of this terrain, this weather. But today he welcomed it. He had a very ancient poem in his Notebook about the human soul setting forth on its final journey across some desolate landscape. In this harshness, this coldness, this loneliness, he felt nearer to Ted, as if he were symbolically keeping faith with him.

He recalled that his foster mother, who, as a Quaker, was not committed to any clear image of an afterlife, had nevertheless harboured a comfortable hope peculiar to herself that the dead might revisit earlier phases and locations of their own lives. For what moral purpose, Joe was not quite sure, but the idea had been vaguely incorporated into his own unbeliever's universe, almost without him realizing it. Now he found himself playing with the thought that Ted's spirit might be even now in Vienna, as if Ted, by dying, had played a neat trick, a philosopher's joke, and got there before him. He almost felt that he might glimpse Ted there next week, getting onto a tram, or strolling ahead in the Stadtpark just too far away to hear . . . Or was Ted safe in unreachable Vienna of before the war? Or was he in some Vienna of both times and all times, his ur-city existing in the mind as much as on the ground – 'not just a place, a whole way of thought and social organization. There was a kind of cult called "Vienna", a belief called "Vienna".'

When Ted speaks – spoke – of Vienna it was as if the city he knew by reputation as a child, and the Imperial capital it had been before his birth, and the city of doom it was to become in his teens, had always co-existed, the past already imbued with a future implicit. And no doubt he was right, for Vienna, for all its vaunted gaiety, was a city with a cult of death in its heart long before the Holocaust. Even the pretty *Wienerisch* wine-tavern songs speak of death when you analyse their words – *Verkauft's mei G'wand, I fahr in Himmel . . . Es wird ein Wein sein, und wir werden nimmer sein:* Off to another place, no future, no time – even to drink this season's wine harvest. Talk about Freud's death wish. Uncle

Sigi sang and hummed and played the banjo: am I inventing it when I think that these were some of his songs?

Today, Vienna's suicide rate is the highest in Europe, I read recently, excepting only that of Budapest, its twin city of Imperial days. And this must long have been true, for, when you think about it, that nineteenth-century tragedy at Mayerling could hardly have sprung unique and unprecedented from the mind of that overwrought but commonplace boy and girl. The heir to the throne, dead by his own hand, and his seventeen-year-old mistress with him: senseless waste and folly . . . Or was it? It was if they were not so much making history as climbing into a historical niche already long prepared for them, mere actors fulfilling a rôle, *La Nuit de Mayerling* long before the event, already there, written.

Others too. Mahler's brother killed himself. So did the poet Georg Trakl, so did Otto Weininger, so did Zweig even though he went across the Atlantic to do it. So did *three* of Wittgenstein's brothers – and so, I seem to remember, did the man who designed the Opera House, of all Viennese institutions. This is ridiculous: suicide itself rendered commonplace, almost cravenly conventional. As with poor Oberst Redl, the ideal, correct, *k und k* officer who was discovered in 1913 to have been a traitor and a homosexual. Was he really either? Perhaps it is more relevant that he was a Jew and of humble origins, facts which he also concealed. But what really horrifies me is that he sat for so many hours in a hotel room being bullied and cajoled by his brother officers before he would consent to place in his brain the traditional, romantically-sanctioned fatal shot.

I do not know how old Redl was when he died, but he had risen to a position of responsibility and influence: I imagine him to have been in middle life, that time of notorious vulnerability and crisis. I see him in my mind as a hidden man behind one of those *Fasching* masks that frightened me when I was very small. Or no, perhaps rather with no face at all, just an empty space beneath his military cap. Like one of those vaguely horrible, semi-human busts of

127

empty armour – helmet, breast plate, crossed swords – that adorn some of the Imperial buildings and the *Gloriette* out at Schönbrunn: ceremonial death as a dark space, an emptiness.

I am afraid. On Sunday night I must get into that train in the valley and be carried off to this city of death where the snow lies pitiless on the dark stone people and where too many other people – my parents, my sister Anna, all my uncles and aunts even to my Uncle Sigi, and now Ted . . . I am afraid.

– And then he said loudly to himself in the biting air: you fool! You bloody fool. You're working yourself into a maudlin state about Vienna, that prosperous, well-lit city with its new metro, where Anna, the living Anna, will come to find you – and all the time what you ought to be afraid of is right here under your skis. Why did you have to come up here this morning? Why did you have to be such a fool?

He had come off the drag-lift into a world of muffled sight and sound. Up on this desolate height the air was white with sleet: he could feel it already beginning to soak into the shoulders of his padded jacket. He could see no more than a few yards all round: the way he must take – the way down the treacherous mountain towards St Wilhelm – was completely invisible. And sound was similarly cut off from him. Now he had left the drag he could not hear its creaking winding-gear: for lack of other custom the wheel must have ceased again. There were no voices, no sounds of other skis on the piste – no one at all here but himself. It was the classic dangerous situation of which he had so often and so sternly warned the children.

He had come up here like a sleepwalker, bent on escape, on getting away from everyone. And now he had, and this was the result. As if it, too, had finally understood, his heart – quiescent all the long ride up – now began to bang in his chest like an independent creature, warning him of what he had done. It pumped so hard it became like a sound in his ears: he thought that anyone standing near him would hear it. But there was no one. Only the snow.

In the silence he began to recite aloud, like a man praying
– but not in supplication, rather in confession and remorse:

> There was a man of double deed
> Sowed his garden full of seed.
> When the seed began to grow
> 'Twas like a garden full of snow.
> When the snow began to melt
> 'Twas like a ship without a belt.
> When the ship began to sail
> 'Twas like a bird without a tail.
> When the bird began to fly
> 'Twas like an eagle in the sky.
> When the sky began to roar
> 'Twas like a lion at the door.
> When the door began to crack
> 'Twas like a stick across my back.
> When my back began to smart
> 'Twas like a penknife in my heart.
> And when my heart began to bleed
> 'Twas death and death and death indeed.

Death indeed. Here up on this mountain where no one knew
he had gone. Well, he had expected it all along. But not so
soon.

He could not see. It maddened him. His goggles seemed
misted, and he pulled them off a moment to wipe them. For
a second, dimly, peering between the flakes of white, he
caught a glimpse, perhaps twenty yards away, of the next
marker pole. Then he narrowed his eyes against the stinging
sleet and it was gone again. But at least it had been there.

He put his goggles back on and blew his nose. His heart,
though still thumping, had calmed itself a little and no longer
seemed likely to burst his chest. He realized that he had a
pressing need to urinate.

Unzipped in the open, whirling snow his own flesh
seemed improbably warm and reassuring: he felt a new,
urgent desire to live. The hot stream drilled into the deep
snow. He perceived himself as, after all, an intricate, subtle

mechanism – heart, lungs, kidneys, digestion, muscles, brain, sexual desire, all working furiously and privately away even in this landscape of ice and invisible precipices. He was a survivor. He *would* survive. What exaggerated, self-fulfilling weakness had just now come over him? What rot – All he had to do was find his way slowly and carefully down to the next marker pole. And then the next.

He set off, feeling his way over the ground like a novice: a little turn here, a small traverse there, a pause to peer again into the whirling dimness yard by yard, almost inch by inch. Once, catching a ski in an invisible hummock, his instant evasive movement almost lost him the ski. He had to take a glove off to readjust it, and then had difficulty getting the glove on again over his chilled fingers. His eyes were watering too with the cold and he had a sudden desire to sit down in the snow and rest . . . No. *No.* That, exactly that, is how it happens.

He was getting on all right, he told himself as he forced a further descent. Getting used to the conditions even. It wasn't too bad if you just kept your head. Just keep your head and tried to feel the lie of the land and not think too much that it might be leading you astray . . . And then he fell heavily, suddenly, he did not even know why. Ice perhaps? Tension seemed to be robbing his legs of their normal intuition. The fall bruised his hip and jarred his whole body. As he lay there a moment, winded, he heard himself moan out loud. Bloody hell. Oh bloody, bloody hell.

Later – quite a bit later, it seemed – he found himself working his way laboriously round the edge of what seemed to be a crater. The way was rough and powdery – had so much more snow really fallen that the piste itself had disappeared? His weak relief on at last coming upon another marker pole and a better defined track was very great. Only afterwards did it occur to him that the number on the poles was now different, and that what he must have done was wandered off the route higher up and made indeed a perilous and unmapped detour round that crater before, by pure good luck, stumbling upon another way down.

And as he felt his way down the invisible mountain, bathed in sweat again now in spite of the cold all round him and the wet snow soaking through his clothes, till at last the snow was less and the grey valley became spectrally visible beneath him, he thought with passionate determination of Anna, the living Anna, whom, by suviving, he would once more hold. To have her once more – just once, even – was now, in weak gratitude at finding himself alive and unharmed, all he asked.

Coming down the last stretch, onto what turned itself into a nursery slope directly above St Wilhelm, no more snow was falling. There were even people about on the hill, misty figures with cheerful shouts. He experienced a numbed surprise at rejoining the human race. It was as if he had been absent, not for hours only, but for much longer, like Thomas the Rhymer returning to the world of men after his sojourn in a land where time runs differently.

It was early in the afternoon, but he was too nervously elated and exhausted to sit here in a café, to eat something. He would ski no more today. He went to the Post Office to wait for the bus back to Heiligenhof. He stood leaning against the shelter enjoying the feeble yellow sun that was now filtering through the snow clouds, the contorted carvings on the gabled house opposite, the feet of small birds making patterns near him in the new film of whiteness. Everything seemed bright, miraculous, intricate, just as it has always been, yet subtly changed as if charged with some inner meaning. Had he finally, by courting disaster but surviving it, left the burden of his angst up on that mountain for good? Ted Litvak knew about that sort of 'epiphany', as he called it. He also, it seemed to Joe, used to refer familiarly to such a crisis as an 'appointment in Samarra': it was one of his intimate shorthand phrases.

Not till he was on the yellow bus and riding home did Joe remember, with a sense of inner recoil, how the story of the appointment in Samarra actually went. He could almost hear Ted's voice, telling it to him.

A man, in the market in Baghdad, glimpsed between the stalls a figure he recognized as Death, coming towards him. Straight away he took the sensible precaution of leaving Baghdad. He journeyed to Samarra, and there felt safe and breathed easily again. But, strolling in the city in the cool of the evening, he encountered Death again, face to face. 'Ah,' said that person, 'I was puzzled to catch sight of you in Baghdad this morning. You see, I knew I had an appointment with you tonight in Samarra.'

To the unseen Ted within him, Joe said now: Do you want to hear about Uncle Sigi in the end? Yes, I'd better tell you. Uncle Sigi's new life did not, after all, turn out the great escape he must have hoped it would be. Like Stefan Zweig, he got clean away from the old country only to be destroyed by the new one. Zweig, as you know, died by his own hand in Brazil in 1942. My Uncle Sigi, as far as I can make out from the sketchy and evasive account I received in the end, did much the same but with less awareness and efficiency. It must have been in the early 1950s that he died of drink in a Home in Seattle run by, of all things, a German Lutheran charity.

So there is no consolation there, Ted; don't try to offer me one. The cost of the New Life is not, as I used dimly to think, the loss of the past, for in the end it turns out the past cannot be lost. No, what is lost is the future, it seems.

6

It had been agreed that on Thursday afternoon, in the last
daylight hours of the old year, the Beech-Lovell tribe should
make an excursion all together. It was Mary, the night
before, who organized them firmly into it. David and Lisette
would just have to get their lesson changed to the morning,
she said, fixing Lisette with her eye, meaning: Female Trades
Union – you make sure he does. And Tom and Joe for once
would have to stop showing off on the high wire and content
themselves with a nice, easy run that all concerned could
manage.

'Huh, look who's talking,' said Tom. 'Show off yourself,
Madam.'

'Suits me,' said Joe. 'I did enough showing off getting
down to St Wilhelm yesterday morning – with no one to
watch me.' He had given a toned-down account of his
exploit in the snow storm, knowing that he must publicly
account for those hours of absence somehow, and for his
own exhaustion, but not wanting to let anyone know the
full extent of his folly. David, in particular, would have
been censorious – rightly so – and Caroline's expression of
strained, suppressed reproach was bad enough anyway: he
did not want it to get worse. He did not, for once, blame
her. To tell your wife hurtful home truths and then to go
out and make what might be construed as a suicidal gesture,
was a low way to behave, there was no doubt of it.

Encouraged by Mary's example of solidarity, he set
himself to be nice to everyone, and to Caroline in particular,
and very nearly succeeded.

On Thursday, they all met for an early lunch as arranged,
not all privately enthusiastic about the afternoon's plan but
acquiescent to it. It was the day when the accumulated
exhaustion of the week's skiing traditionally catches up with
the visitor, the day when the holiday has passed its prime
and is suddenly perceived as declining towards its ending.

On Friday and Saturday, gripped by a renewed desire not to waste time, by then running out fast, they would bestir themselves to fresh efforts and challenges, but today there seemed to have been a general slackening. Even Mary, normally indefatigable, admitted that she had divided the morning between reading her stack of children's books and casing the village's three sportswear shops for a new sweater.

'Oh, Joe and I spent half the morning in the bar at the top of the cabin lift, didn't we Joe?' said Tom, not to be outdone. Joe agreed, though it wasn't entirely true. The fact was, he had felt so depleted in energy that he had simply followed, for once, wherever Tom had wanted to go. He had also, in his weakness, confided in Tom alone the full extent of his yesterday's ordeal.

'Sounds quite nasty,' Tom had simply commented, and bought him another beer. Among Tom's equivocal virtues, Joe had long known, were a lack of moral stance toward the behaviour of others, and an ability to keep his mouth shut when requested that belied his usual lack of tact.

It appeared that David, Lisette and Jerome, suddenly possessed with an infantile urge, had rented toboggans that morning and had careered riotously up and down the slope set aside for the sport amid crowds of smaller boys and girls.

'Oh it was so funny, racing,' said Lisette. 'We laughed and laughed! And we kept falling off the toboggans. I'm covered in bruises now, much more than I ever get from skiing. Mummy'll wonder, when I get home, if someone's been beating me up!'

Caroline, Joe saw, looked as if she were wincing faintly at this remark. Lisette herself seemed innocently unaware that a sexual innuendo might be construed from it. Would she let her mother know that David was her lover? Or would she just assume that her mother had understood that fact? Or would she, on the other hand, count on her mother *not* having understood it, and on Joe and Caroline not informing on her? But no, he did not think, from the way Lisette spoke, that she had that sort of secret from her mother. Not for the first time, he wondered how she and David envisaged

134

their joint future, if indeed they did. In their room in the chalet were they concocting a private world of hopes and dreams, imaginary children even, colonizing the future as he himself had helplessly tended to do whenever his affections were engaged? Or were they, of another generation from himself and freer, content just to enjoy the present as young, healthy creatures? Possibly David, a boy of nineteen with his life still to make, might be capable of such disassociation, but he doubted if Lisette was. For all her childish directness, she seemed to him emotionally fully formed. He guessed that David's attentions to her had awakened in her already a response of defenceless commitment, making their relationship for her a marriage in miniature. He hoped quite desperately that his son would recognize the quality of this love and not devalue it by betrayal. Once you began to debase the currency of caring –

'Weren't you able to change your lesson to the morning, then?' asked Caroline.

'Didn't try,' said David provocatively. 'We all wanted to toboggan, didn't we Lizzie?'

'Yes, but don't call me Lizzie,' said Lisette spiritedly. 'It makes me feel as if I were someone else.'

'Oh, who?' asked Mary Lovall, as if suddenly scenting a fictional theme.

'Oh – someone skinny, I think. And sort of cross. Oh dear! Actually I could do with being a bit skinnier. I've put on weight this week in spite of the skiing. My tummy's fat. It's all this lovely food.' Indeed the only faint fault Joe could perceive in Lisette was that she was a little greedy.

'Or else it's love,' said Tom sentimentally and facetiously. There was a general, self-conscious laugh, and Lisette went pink.

'Nonsense, dear, you're just right,' said Caroline automatically. She was still pursuing the children's missed lesson. 'It seems a pity,' she murmured, 'When you've paid for it.'

'Oh Mu-um!' David reverted to the indignant whine he had picked up at primary school. 'Don't go on so. Give it a rest. It's only one lesson. It's not a vast sum. Anyone would think you were mean all through about money to hear the way you carry on. It's lucky we know you're not.' It was Caroline's turn to flush.

'Well I missed mine too,' said Jerome.

'I noticed,' said Caroline primly. Implication: you're not my son so I'm not going to reproach you, but really I do think it's a bit much the levity with which you all treat that ski school.

'Yes, I'm sorry to leave you to it, Caroline,' Jerome went on boldly, suddenly finding the placatory manner of an older man, 'but honestly I'm not sure I can stand the class any more. You know, this happens to me every holiday. Class wimp, that's me. And once I've established that rôle it really seems better to retire. So I think, if you don't mind, I'll leave you and the others to those bloody parallel turns tomorrow. You're all so much better than me.'

'But what will you do?' asked Caroline, sounding bereft. Joe guessed that Jerome had been rehearsing his little speech; she might at least let him go gracefully, he thought, with his customary reflex of irritation, but in the same moment perceived Caroline's aloneness like a small pain in his own heart.

He had hardly exchanged two words alone with her since his explosion of the previous morning: the night had been passed in coma as far as he was concerned, a space of blackness into which he had fallen gratefully like a man giving himself up to an inevitable fate. No wonder he felt today as if he were still not properly round from an anaesthetic.

'I shall trundle up and down the nice nursery slope enjoying myself for once,' Jerome answered firmly.

'I bet you don't, I bet you sneak back to that book shop!' said David, laughing, not unkindly.

'Yes, trust Jerome to find a book shop,' said Lisette. 'It's in the big, posh hotel – no, not the one at the top of the lift, but the grand one at the end of the village on the far side of the church. We went there this morning because it's got an indoor swimming pool and we thought we might go there after skiing today.'

'What does the pool look like?'

'Oh *lovely* – isn't it, David? But it's awfully expensive, so I'm not sure we'll go. I suppose it has to be, for people who aren't staying there, or everyone would want to use it. It's got a sauna and a jacuzzi and everything too.'

'Oh really? *I* might go,' said Mary. 'I like a sauna and I haven't had one in ages. Frightfully good for elderly strained muscles. Want to join me, Caroline?'

Caroline said she'd never tried one, she wasn't sure she'd like it.

'Shall we make a move?' said Tom, impatient.

As Mary and Joe rode up the mountain together in the chair lift she suddenly placed a hand on his knee.

'How are you?'

'OK – I think. How are you?'

'Oh – me, I'm all right,' said Mary, in the brisk tone of one who does not welcome such an inquiry. After a minute, she continued:

'You looked last night as if you'd seen a ghost.'

'Perhaps I had.' He gazed into the bright, low, afternoon sun.

'You don't want to play tricks with mountains at our age,' she said softly. 'We haven't the stamina any more.'

'How did you – ? Did Tom – ?' But no, Tom would have had no opportunity to pass on this morning's confidence.

'Nope. I just guessed. Oh Joe! Do take care.'

'I'm here,' he said, briefly taking her hand. 'I'm here. So it's all right, isn't it?'

After another space of time Mary said, as if with a disjointed telepathy:

'It all seems so real and present, doesn't it? The village, I mean, and the lifts and the ski runs and the chalet and those jolly girls and all the other people in charge and the rescue services – all busily working away as if we had nothing to do for ever and ever but get up each morning and flog up and down snow precipices and then stuff ourselves with food at night and fall asleep. But in three days time – no, less –

137

it's all going to disappear. The whole village will be packed away like a toy, the mountains will be rolled up like a map – and we'll be on our own again.'

'I know just what you mean.'

They rode for half a minute in companionable silence. Then Mary said, mocking, self-deprecatingly –

'Rather an egocentric view of an entire place, I do admit.'

'Oh God,' he said laughingly, 'if you and I can't share a little cosy egocentricity, who can? I can go further than that, anyway. Skiing villages themselves know they're toys, to be laid out and put away again for other people's use, but I can play that game with virtually anywhere. I remember once taking off from Washington, going back to England, and flying over its suburbs with an absolutely clear impression that the Giants in Charge were already picking up the matchbox houses and stacking those little blue oval mats – '

After a momentary pause for concentration, Mary said: 'Swimming pools.'

'Quite.'

'Oh, I feel exactly the same about America. It's always too – fabulous, somehow. It always was, wasn't it? The New World. And today I suppose we hear too much about it, and see it too often on film, before we ever go there. So we never believe that the real thing *is* quite real.'

'Yes, but the point is,' Joe persisted, 'you can feel that *any* place you only occasionally visit has been dismantled and put away – or I can – and yet by the same token it seems potentially always accessible. Because out of normal time, you see. As if it were just stacked away at the back of a – a wardrobe or somewhere. Invisible but quite near to hand.'

'You've been reading those children's books by C. S. Lewis.'

'Have I?'

'A magic country that you reach by going through the back of a wardrobe. Didn't you read them to your children when they were small?'

'I don't remember. And I think I would have registered a

138

story like that.' The secret room, he thought, with a sudden clutch of longing. The secret room. Behind the sliding panel Flaubert's royal chamber of the heart.

'The magic land is called Narnia,' said Mary, momentarily assuming her rôle as an authority on children's literature. 'But there are other ways to get there besides the wardrobe, as far as I remember. You can cross the Wood between the Worlds. And time runs differently there, as in the myths about fairyland.'

He thought how Vienna, of no time and all time, was even now, across the mountains of Austria, being assembled for him.

' – Actually,' Mary was continuing sententiously, 'I think that, like all the folk tales about fairyland, Narnia is another fable of death. C. S. Lewis's mother died when he was only a child – '

'Look,' said Joe suddenly, not wanting to listen any more, peering over the edge of the chair. 'From here you can see already that it's all a toy.' Sure enough, Heiligenhof was spread out in minature beneath them. The Meccano towers of the big lifts, and the intricate tiny wires and winding wheels of the drags, seen together in perspective, gave the model an oddly industrial look, as if all that energy being expended by the circling stick-figures on the slopes were linked to some overall enterprise of production.

'Hey, what do I see on that further drag?' said Mary. 'Isn't it – ?'

'Yup. Blood wagon being taken up. Someone at the top there must have had an accident.'

Two stick insects in the dark red worn by the Heiligenhof ski instructors were riding up the lift with a long covered stretcher balanced between them. The low sun glinted with a momentary flash on the buckles of its straps.

'It always looks so horribly coffin-like,' said Mary.

'Doesn't it? But it might be going up for nothing more than a sprained knee, you know. That drag goes up to an awkward run with no other way down, I think.' He sensed that Mary and he both felt uneasy, as at a bad omen.

'Typical,' she said. 'An afternoon towards the end of the week, I mean, when everyone's getting tired or over-confident. Just when accidents happen.'

'Mmm.' He did not want to talk about it.

'And New Year's Day tomorrow,' she persisted. 'Something dodgy, I always think, about the New Year. I don't trust it. It pretends to be a lovely fresh start. But it isn't, and if you behave as if it is then it's likely to get its own way back on you.'

'There aren't any fresh starts.'

'Quite. And the one time I convinced myself there were and made a resolution that the New Year would be different – it *was* different. Something awful happened.' Her voice quivered fractionally.

He turned towards her then, knowing in reawakened dread that he ought to ask her 'what?' But the chairs were reaching the lift-station.

Caroline, having got off the chair with Tom ahead of the others, said:

'I do hope I can manage this run.'

He didn't hear her and she repeated it. He looked at her in apparently genuine incomprehension:

'Why shouldn't you. It's not complicated.'

'Oh Tom, you don't realize . . . I'm *not a good skier*. I've really made no progress at all this week. Sometimes I think I should just give it up.'

'Oh I shouldn't do that,' said Tom amiably, fiddling with his boot.

'Why?' she challenged him. He had to think then.

'Well . . . It'd be a bit hard on Joe, wouldn't it? I mean, he enjoys it so much.'

'Well he could still go. With you, or – ' Anna Morley. Setting off for a jolly holiday with the Lovells and without me. Two pairs.

Oh no, that mustn't happen, it mustn't, I can't let it. Tom is right, even if he doesn't know why. I have to keep on coming on these exhausting, nerve-racking holidays, at least until – until when? Until what? I don't know. I am waiting for something, nerves taut. But I don't know what it is. I am afraid. He is frightening me. Joe is.

'You'll manage this run,' said Tom consolingly. 'You're probably tired, that's all. We're all a bit tired today. Tell you what, you stick behind me and I'll give you a lead down and if I'm going too fast for you just give a shout and I'll slow down, mmm?'

'Oh Tom, you are *kind*,' she said, meaning it. Mary's lucky to have him, really, for all he can be a bit irritating sometimes. I'm not sure she really appreciates him enough. It tried to tell her that two years ago, when she was in that peculier state and talking about leaving him. We should all count our blessings. Joe and *I* should, I know – though he's too silly to realize it. He's so destructive, critical. There's something working within him, almost at times as if he is trying to destroy us, himself . . . Oh, but he can't be, why should he? There's no reason, no sense in it. I mustn't think like that, even to think about it is dangerous. I won't. I *won't*. He's been nice today. But the way he was yesterday morning . . . Like someone *possessed*. Such an enemy. My enemy. He frightens me. Where is he trying to take me – himself? Oh God, please God, don't let him do anything – horrible. No – no, think about better, more positive things. About Jenn and David turning out so well on the whole. About sitting in Court on a good day, feeling you're doing something that matters and that, even if everyone concerned isn't exactly satisfied at the end of it at least you've tried to be fair. I've always wanted things to be like that, ever since I was a child. Not marvellous, no, I don't seem to be very good at marvellous. Just fair.

What else? Think about not dying of cancer, about having friends and enough money, about Tom being nice to me . . .

'We off then?' said Tom as the party stood assembled. 'OK chaps: Joe you lead – but do spare a thought for the rest of us.'

'The weaker brethren,' intoned Jerome. His father ignored him.

'Caro'? You follow me, love, like I said. David, Lisette – all set? Right!'

Joe first, then Mary, then David and Lisette disappeared alarmingly over the top, down the first steep, short slope to the first wide plateau. Tom followed, waving Caroline down after him. She negotiated the first slope with conscious, ski-lesson care, saying to herself 'Fair . . . blessings . . . blessings . . . fair.' At the end of the troupe, more clumsily, came Jerome.

Predictably, Joe and Mary descended the top part of the run with unthinking ease and then had to pull up on a hillock in a hidden valley to wait for the others. It was cold but clear. The fresh snow of yesterday's storm lay dazzlingly unsullied in spite of a morning's use. Their breath steamed a little.

'So, what nasty trick did that other New Year play on you?' Joe asked abruptly. After all, he found he wanted to know. Someone else's map might be a help. You never knew.

'Oh – that. Yes. Well, not so much a nasty trick, more a sort of retribution. I'd – I'd expected something momentous, you see. Tom and I weren't getting on too well and he was away a lot. (I think he was having one of his things with some dreary little secretary, actually) but I was working like a demon and had just been invited to go on that lecture tour in the States. I had that scary but exciting walking-on-the-edge-of-something feeling. I was all strung up. I thought that perhaps everything – my life, you know, was due for some sort of major shift . . . Oh, God knows what I thought, some conceited fantasy of my own power and importance, I dare say.' She paused, and he knew she would not spell out her then-fantasy any more clearly. It was over.

'But what happened?' he persisted.

'Oh – yes. Sorry. Well I think you know about it, actually. In May the year before last. My goddaughter Sandy.'

'She died, didn't she, in some sort of tragedy?' said Joe. 'Of course I remember.'

'Drowned. Sailing with two friends, another girl and a boy. The others were saved. She was seventeen.' Her face was turned from him, but he heard her voice was suddenly rough with tears.

'Mary, I'm so sorry. I remember of course hearing about it at the time. But I didn't realize – '

'That I would mind so much?' said Mary implacably. 'No, in theory and in prospect *I* wouldn't have said such an event, however distressing, would have affected me, personally, quite so hard. I always thought I had a good creative writer's carapace of selfishness and separateness to protect me from absolute grief. But – oh Joe, when it actually happened it seemed just *so awful*, I can't tell you, and still does. Like some bloody great scythe ripping through the whole fabric of life, calling everything into question, making a nonsense of it all. It wasn't just a life destroyed, it was a whole future, and her parents' future too – she was an only child. And she was such a love and so intelligent. Oh, I'm sorry, I'll stop in a minute, but I still cry whenever I think of it, it's as if the tears are coming from some water main right down inside me and I don't have any control of them.' She tore off her goggles and glasses and mopped her face, still turned from him.

'You said "retribution" a minute ago,' said Joe humbly, after a moment. 'Did you think that life was sort of – paying you back for expecting something exciting to happen?'

'Momentous, I said, rather than exciting. Well, yes, I was being paid back, but it was more as if – as if something in me *had actually foreseen* this terrible life-stopping event, but I had conceitedly misinterpreted it as something more general to do with myself. It – the tragedy – had been there all the time, coming, you see, like a sort of threatening hum below the horizon, and *that* was what I had been picking up and misinterpreting.' She replaced her goggles with an air of closing the subject.

He said, very surprised: 'But Mary – you, of all people, surely don't believe that?'

'Why not?' she said briskly, giving her nose a final blow. She still did not look at him.

'I dunno, but . . . You're too sane, I would have thought. I supposed I was the only person around obsessed enough really to believe that the future is there waiting for us.'

'What's not sane about that?'

'Well – free will . . .'

'What's so sane about the theory of free will? It may turn out to be as groundless and sentimental a western prejudice as – as the Virgin Birth or the doctrine of Redemption or any other rot. Why, look at your own family background: look at the Holocaust. One in the eye for the free will theory, I'd have said, wouldn't you? Six million people, all on an inexorable conveyor belt, long before they knew it. Condemned already, while they were still living comfortable lives in those European cities. Sitting on sofas and riding on trams and already as good as dead. Auschwitz and Dachau all the time waiting for them.'

She ended on a high tone as if she would say more, but did not. After a long moment, Joe said:

'I can't argue with you, Mary. I agree with you.'

She turned to look at him then, but behind her goggles he could not see her eyes. 'Oh Joe – I shouldn't really go on like this. To you of all people. I'm sorry. And in any case it's all immaterial, because we still have to live "as if", don't we?'

'As if we had free will?'

'Yes. We have no realistic alternative . . . Oh bugger this, I'm getting cold. Where the hell are the rest of them?'

David and Lisette had arrived on the scene several minutes before, but had stayed some way off on the gentle slope playing ski-leapfrog. The other three had not yet appeared round the side of a bluff.

'I expect my poor old Jerome's managed to lose a ski again,' Mary said, with a weak giggle.

But Joe was now watching Lisette, and fear gripped him.

All the time waiting. Sudden, choking, sweating fear, worse even than the snow storm, worse than on the plane at the beginning of the week, as bad as if Lisette, Lisette . . . Lisette motionless, crushed, broken, defiled. Robbed of life.

She danced in his vision, pink-and-blue, like a figure in a snowstorm ball. He could not reach her. He could not save her.

He moaned, perhaps audibly, and must have reached toward Mary as if supplicating her help, for she put out her mitt to grasp his.

'Oh Joe, what is it?'

'Lisette . . .' He said, and then, with a great effort, 'No, I think I really mean – Anna.'

'Anna? Anna Morley?'

They stared at each other, hands clutched, in mutual distress and incomprehension. At last Mary said gently:

'I – I do know about you and Anna, of course. Actually she told me herself. But I don't think we ought to talk about it. Not now, I mean.'

'Anna Morley?' he said wildly. He had literally forgotten about her during their last conversation. 'No, no, not her. My sister. My sister Anna.'

But then Tom was there, and Caroline and Jerome, skiing right up and stopping in a flurry of powder snow, (Jerome nearly fell over) and Tom was saying testily, as if the delay were everyone's fault but his:

'*There* you are. Come on, let's get on for God's sake. The sun's sinking. At this rate it'll've gone before we get down.'

The rift valley narrowed and deepened into a long coomb, ending in a brief rise up again to a crest before a further sharp descent. The light was milky, the sun a red ball.

Joe skied alone and in torment.

Retribution. Isn't that really what I fear? Retribution for my saved life, all my good fortune and the hubris and carelessness it has begotten. Retribution for not having gone into that abyss where the others went, where my father went at the age I am now, where Uncle Sigi went in his own way

145

though he fled to the far rim of the New World in a vain attempt to avoid it?

If my father and mother and the rest of them died, not from any thorough-going sin or offence but simply from ignorance and a failure in imagination, then how much greater retribution is due to me? I have none of their excuses, I am a generation later than them; I know more than they did – and they are what I know. For the retribution exacted by Fate goes beyond any judgement of a court of law, far beyond the civilized decencies of the Christian ethic; to Fate, 'fair' is a concept with no meaning. Anna – Anna Morley – knows that. Oh, remember her haemorrhage of tears in that basement beneath my office, when that deformed green creature with the tiny head drew itself again and again on the lighted screen. And her saying 'I wanted him originally. I wanted him very much. Where did I go wrong just in indulging in the sort of cosy, self-centred desire for a child that everyone has?'

But there is worse than that, even. There is the retribution that reaches you via another person, a truly innocent one, who pays the price instead of you. Oh, I know that Anna and Aidan's boy is 'innocent', in the oldest sense of the word, but he is unfeeling, unknowing: just an undeveloped brain in a lolling body to be fed slops, cleaned of shit, for ever and ever; one cannot say that he suffers, that he knows what life is to lose. But Anna, my sister Anna, the other Anna I carry within me – she knew.

She was seventeen when they came for her. The same age as Mary's goddaughter, younger even than Lisette. She, with her masses of hair, lovely, thick, undisciplined, Jewish hair, like in the Klimt paintings in our mother's book, was picked up in the street, it seems. My one tiny hope in this darkest level of the abyss is that our mother and father never knew for certain of her fate. But I have to know it, because an overworked and ill-advised man from an international agency in Vienna told me, when I was foolhardy enough to go to his office and ask, one day about ten years ago.

Anna my sister was taken to the Gestapo headquarters on

Franz Josef Kai, beneath the medieval Jewish quarter, almost within a stone's throw of Stefansdom. There she suffered a fate that, even in that place and time, was not quite ordinary. She was raped many times before being strung up in a posture of crucifixion in an inner courtyard for a night and a day and a night. It was summer, and hot. No water, nothing, not even myrrh. No, I cannot really follow her there in spirit, however much I think I should. On the lip of that precipice my imagination fails. But I have to know the facts. And, no, the SS did not leave a written record of this: even their bureaucratic efficiency did not extend that far. But another prisoner, who saw her and knew her name, lived till after the war, and he told the international agency who wrote it in their records and, years later, told me.

Ted Litvak once said that, since the war, the phrase 'a beautiful Jewish girl' had become a pornographic one, so loaded is it with the implication of defilements committed or salaciously contemplated. After my visit to the agency I understood what he meant. I think the harassed, unwise official even used the phrase to me. Apologetically. Categorizing. Cretinous oaf. And yet, and yet . . . No, he was right to tell me. I deserved to know. Why should I be spared that?

And afterwards? She is 'believed to have been' transported eastwards. If she survived her abyss. I do not even know that. The trail goes dead, after that. Not even a place name to lay over her memory.

They pulled down the block on Franz Josef Kai, after the war. I went to see. Where else could I go? In its place is a dank garden beneath a surviving rampart of the old city wall, and there used to be a rather circumspect and uninformative plaque but even that has now gone. I think the Viennese are a bit ashamed of what went on there. But not too much, because they never are. Who was it said that the Austrians make poor Nazis but good anti-Semites? And anyway guilt and death have long been institutionalized, in Vienna, and absorbed into its traditions, coarsened and romanticized, like the carnival masks, or the *Schadenfreude* of the *Heurigen* songs.

He reached the crest, slipped over it, and began the sharper descent. The bright afternoon had paled now into a hint of mist. He was ahead of all the others. He skied without thought, his mind several hundred miles and a night in a train away: he was in a high building in the dark zero-city of his dreams. Hidden within it. In a hotel somewhere in the Old City, looking inwards into a ravine of a courtyard where snow fell and fell forever beyond the double windows. Safe forever. Or in the equally high, enclosing building on Franz Josef Kai, with the other Anna, the first Anna: another sort of secret room. '*That dark and vicious place* . . .' Room 101. A place of unimaginable retribution.

Which?

He had reached another plateau before he became aware of voices calling him.

'Dad . . . Joe . . . Dad! . . .' David and Lisette.

He skidded to a stop, swung round, and found to his surprise they were close behind him. He had heard nothing.

'Christ, are you *deaf*, Dad? We've been yelling our heads off.' David, agitated and red in the face.

'Oh Joe, please come back,' Lisette, without her cap, hair – lovely, undisciplined hair – tumbling, an air of distress.

'What is it? Has someone – ?'

'It's Jerome,' said David heavily. 'Look – up there.'

Joe peered up at the slope he had descended unthinkingly a few minutes before, and was surprised to find how steep and narrow it now looked. One-third the way down it, like flies stuck to a high, white wall, were four stick-figures: Tom, Mary, Caroline and, sitting down, Jerome.

'Why can't he get down?'

'He could've,' said David wearily. 'Mum was managing all right. But it's a bit icy and Jerome just lost his nerve and stuck. Then Tom shouted at him, so he went all stubborn.'

Joe could imagine the scene all too well. There had been analogous ones at intervals throughout Jerome's childhood.

'I'd better go back with you and see if I can talk him down,' he said.

'It's a bit late for that. He's hurt himself.'

'He did get moving in the end,' said Lisette, biting her lips in distress. 'Tom was so horrid to him. But that wasn't sensible of Tom because Jerome got angry too, and the very first turn he did, he fell, almost as if he were showing Tom. And now he's hurt.'

'We think,' said David, ' – Mum and Mary think – that he's bust his collarbone.'

So that was it. Jerome. Not David, or Lisette, but Jerome. And not dead but just a broken bone. A disaster but not a tragedy. A selfish, grateful flood of relief and anti-climax enveloped him.

'Do you want me up there? – No, I'd better ski on down and get a stretcher sent up, hadn't I?'

'That was the idea of chasing after you, Dad.'

'Right.' He collected his wits a moment. 'David, will you climb back up to them and tell them I'm on my way to set things in motion. Lisette – no sense in you hauling yourself up there again too, you come on down with me.' It was rather that he wanted her company, though (as he realized guiltily as soon as David had left them) he would have got down quicker on his own.

Over the next ridge the toy Heiligenhof appeared again, dimly, far below them, improbable source of stretchers, doctors, hospitals. It now seemed infinitely desirable.

Down at last in the village made real, the mist was rising. Joe located the Mountain Rescue Post. There was a covered stretcher available, like the one that had seen being taken up the mountain an hour or so before, but two others were already called out with their teams in different directions, the worried attendant said. It had been an afternoon for accidents – 'ein Nachmittag voll Unfälle' – and he was short of manpower. If he found one man, could Joe help get the stretcher up the mountain and to the right spot? The Post would try to radio for a second mountain guide to meet

149

them up there, but if one could not be summoned Joe might also have to help in bringing the injured person down.

'I can manage that,' said Joe. He felt calm now, and confident as he had not done for a long time.

The man still looked worried, but Lisette, appealed to in English, insisted on Joe's expertise. A spare ski instructor was hastily summoned, and Joe and he prepared to set off for the main cabin lift with the stretcher between them. Lisette looked very distressed again at the sight of it.

'Oh *poor* Jerome, I'm sure he's in bad pain. Oughtn't you to have something to give him?'

'Look, all here. Morphine is.' The instructor tapped a corner of the covers. 'And *Schiene*. Bandages. Everything. No worry.'

'That's why it's called a blood wagon, my love.'

When they had embarked in the cabin which had been summarily cleared for them, a little hush of awe and anxiety falling on the cheerful crowd as they moved out of the way. Joe looked back. Lisette was still standing by the foot of the lift looking forlorn, as if she felt she had abandoned Jerome.

They had to take the stretcher up to a high point and then ski with it down by a lateral route to where Jerome and the others were stuck. Joe saw with relief, as they came over the ridge at last, that the small party, now joined by several other passing skiers, had somehow got Jerome down from the steepest slope onto a gentler one. In spite of his claim to competence, he had been uncertain how he and his companion would load a helpless person onto the stretcher while balanced on such a slope. It was very cold now, and the light, even up on the mountain, was beginning to fade.

When they got to him, Jerome, skis off, was sitting slumped on the hard-packed snow, his face drawn with pain. He was being exhorted by an unknown couple, and an instructor with a walkie-talkie who had evidently been directed there. After all, the wild mountains were colonized, thought Joe in hazy thankfulness: they were mapped and patrolled; people in uniform were in charge of them. Caroline, voluble with relief at the presence now of two instructors, was there also. Tom and Mary, however, stood some way off, and without even hearing their voices Joe saw that they were engaged in a row.

'He has his collarbone broken,' the walkie-talkie instructor informed him.

'Yes, that's what we thought – ' But Joe could see that he himself had now become abruptly redundant. The two men in red took over: Jerome was given a shot of morphine, and his distressed face relaxed after a few moments into a foolish smile. He was strapped onto the sledge, with hearty Austrian jokes, covered with blanket and canvas, and his new guardians were away with him down the mountain almost before Mary had realized that her son was going and came floundering sideways up the slope, skis splayed.

'Too busy talking about what's wrong with me even to notice what's happening to him, huh?' said Tom loudly and nastily.

Mary turned round, staggered back again, her fury rendered slow-motion by the terrain, and slapped Tom's face hard. The sound rang in the icy, silent air.

'Oh Mary, *don't*,' cried Caroline superfluously.

'*That's* for what you did to Jerome, you fat, sadistic oaf,' Mary screamed at her husband.

The unknown couple who witnessed this exuded a civilized but scandalized disgust. The woman shuffled nervously away as if about to leave the scene at once, but the man said 'Now, now!' loudly and made a crabwise move towards Tom, with the air of a responsible citizen about to break up a fight in a pub. He was, however, a good many feet away. Tom, meanwhile, lunged towards Mary as if about to hit her back, but caught one ski across the other and collapsed heavily onto the ground, skis waving, thereby converting the scene from melodrama to near-farce. The other woman drew in her breath sharply. Joe had an insane desire to laugh.

But Mary was in tears, so he slid rapidly down the slope to her, and conveyed her with him a further ten yards off out of Tom's range. He placed himself between her and the rest of the party.

'What on earth's that all about? . . . Come on, love, blow your nose, use my hanky.'

Mary blew obediently like a furious child, but continued to sob:

'He's a bastard. He's cruel and stupid and always has been.'

'Mary, Mary – don't, love. Jerome's going to be all right.'

'You didn't see, you were already further on, it was after Jerome fell. Tom told him to get up again, and Jerome was sitting there and saying "Oh my arm, my arm" and *obviously* in pain, and Tom just took no notice and grabbed him, right by his hurt shoulder, and tried to pull him up. Jerome was screaming in agony and that oaf didn't stop – your David had to pull him off. I'd like to kill him. Tom, I mean.'

'You don't mean that.'

'Yes I do. Or really hurt him, as he's hurt Jerome – and I *don't* mean just now. I mean all the other ways in which he's hurt Jerome too, ever since Jerome began to grow up. Going on at him and jeering at him and wanting him to be different and athletic – and recently why doesn't he have a girlfriend and so on – Oh, he's so stupid, it makes me sick, he understands nothing.'

At a loss to calm her, Joe said: 'All right, love, all right, I know he's a bit crass. But he isn't an ogre, and I have seen him be a good father to Jerome too. All the Meccano they used to do together . . . I was never any good at that, with David, when he was younger.'

'Well, he's no bloody good now. Oh, he pretends to be joking, "just teasing" – *you* know – but he's harassing the boy. And so, because of Tom, Jerome comes home as little as he can, and once he leaves Oxford he won't come home at all and I'll hardly ever see him, and I'll just be alone with that bloody oaf for ever and ever.' She burst into fresh tears.

Joe, feeling someone near him, turned round prepared to shield Mary from a further physical assault. Tom was indeed standing there, stony-faced, but flanked by an escort of Caroline and the unknown man.

'Caroline says,' said Tom with extreme coldness, 'that I

should apologize for trying to get Jerome up like that. All right, I apologize. I didn't realize he was hurt.'

'And I'm sure that Mary – ' Caroline began, but was quelled by a look from Joe.

'Ah well, these things will happen,' said the other man loudly and absurdly. 'Least said, soonest mended, eh? And now I suggest to you good people that we all get down the mountain while there's still some light to see by.'

They descended, a subdued, wide-spaced group, David balancing Jerome's skis across his shoulder. By and by Caroline came alongside Joe and said:

'Poor Mary . . . I suppose all that was really because she was upset at Jerome being hurt?'

'I suppose so too.' He did not feel inclined to offer a different view. Caroline might, in fact, be right. After a moment he asked: 'Was Tom really rough with him?'

'I didn't actually *see* it. I was a bit behind when Jerome first fell, and concentrating hard on staying upright myself. And then everything happened quickly . . . But I know that Mary minds frightfully Jerome growing up. She puts on such a good act one doesn't realize it, but she does mind.'

He said: 'Don't we all. Mind them growing up, I mean. We *all* try to put on a good act. Don't we? And then when something like this happens, the act caves in . . .'

She nodded, and swallowed, and they skied slowly side by side for a little way. When they paused on a knoll – Joe had waited for her to reach it – she said in a thin, high voice:

'I know it sounds silly. But sometimes when I shut my eyes I can almost feel their hands as they used to be in mine, all small like children's hands are. Or the backs of their heads when walking along. Or on my lap after a bath, like little rabbits . . . Even when they are actually with us, and grown up as they are today, I still sometimes get these feelings of longing for them as they were.'

'I know. *Those* children have gone.'

'Yes. Gone forever. It's – it's almost as if they *died*. Oh dear, I shouldn't say that, I know we're lucky really – '

153

'Don't bother with that,' said Joe passionately, 'it *is* as if they've died. I know exactly what you mean. One isn't allowed to complain. But actually it's terrifying.'

Have I been so dreading that something terrible will happen because, in the profound illogical core where parental love has its being, I think that something terrible *has* already happened? The disaster of loss, unformulated but with many possible faces, that we fugitively dreaded all the years we were rearing the children, has, by terrible, anodyne sleight of hand come all the same. With concentration and prudence and luck we avoided it – only to meet it again in another guise round the final corner. Our children have gone. And the nice but busy and competitive adults who have replaced them are no substitute. It's just this: the ultimate, inevitable betrayal of love, of care. Nothing more.

For a minute he and Caroline lingered together on the knoll, looking at each other, as if each would say more but neither could find the words. Joe suddenly shivered.

'Don't get cold,' said Caroline. 'You've had a whole extra run, up and down this mountain. You go on at your own pace. I'll take my time.'

'Sure?'

'Quite sure.'

He smiled, touched her arm, and went. After a couple of turns he sighted David, encumbered with the extra skis, making wide, slow sweeps further down the slope; he sped down to join him.

'Hi, Dad.'

'Hi . . . I'm tired.'

'So'm I. It was really cold hanging around up there waiting for you to turn up with the other guy. Was it difficult, skiing with that stretcher thing?'

'Not really. Once I'd got the hang of it.'

'Mmm . . . Where will they have taken Jerome?'

'To St Wilhelm, the chap said. There's a cottage hospital there, apparently. They'll keep him for the night. I should

154

think the local doctors are pretty good at plastering broken bones, wouldn't you?'

'I should think so . . . Poor old Jerome, though. Will he be able to come back with us on Sunday?'

'I hope so. I expect so.'

After a minute David asked: 'Where did Lisette go, Dad?'

'Back to the chalet, I should imagine. Unless she's hung about to see Jerome brought down safely.'

'She probably did that. She's fond of Jerome. She was awfully upset at what happened.'

'So I saw.' Shocked too, I dare say, he thought, if what Mary said was anything like true. He wanted to ask David about it, but the boy had tacked off at an angle, Jerome's skis awkward across his shoulder. After a moment, Joe saw he was making for the intermediate lift-station. He hastened after him.

'Dad? . . . I'm going down the rest of the way in the chair, I think. I feel weighted down. And I want to see that Lisette's OK.'

'I'll come with you. Give those skis to me now, if you want.'

In the chair beside his father, David said spontaneously:

'It's mostly Tom's fault – that poor old Jerome's hurt, you know.'

'So I gather.'

'Jerome was being pretty annoying, I know. He daydreams, I think, doesn't look where he's going, and then panics when he finds himself in a tight place. But Tom shouldn't have lost his temper.'

'That's what Mary said. More or less.'

'He kept standing over Jerome saying sarkily "Don't be so bloody wet." Well, Jerome is wet at skiing, but so what? It's no good telling someone not to be wet, it makes them wetter. Anyway, he's not wet in other ways. He's a fantastic driver.'

'So I gather. That's a thought, actually, he won't be able to drive his car for a bit. You three'll have to alter your plans when you get back to London, I'm afraid.'

'Mmm,' said David dejectedly. He obviosuly did not want to think about the holiday ending. After a minute Joe said tentatively:

'Mary seemed to think that this – this accident – was the result of a lot of things, not just Jerome's bad skiing. She says Tom's always getting at him. Do you think that's true? I always thought that Tom was a pretty good father when you were all small.'

'Oh – then,' said David, as if glancing down a vista into an impossibly remote period. But after a long pause he added:

'Tom's all right in his way. I mean, he's quite generous. I'd get on with him OK, I think, if he were my dad. You just don't want to take him too seriously. But he and Jerome – they just aren't suited to one another somehow. Jerome's too clever and too sensitive. He sets off something nasty in Tom. Tom's a bit of a Fifth Form bully. You know what I mean?'

'Yes. Yes, I do.'

'And,' added David in an elaborately offhand tone, 'Jerome being gay, of course, doesn't help. I think it's really that that's getting under Tom's skin.'

In the loaded silence that followed, Joe felt his mental landscape jolt and shift as in a minature landslide, settling into a slightly new contour. The word gay – so inappropriate, in its basic sense, to Jerome's own lugubrious brand of irony – danced madly in his mind. For a while he did not speak. David, made uneasier by this, said truculently:

'You knew that, I daresay?'

'No, actually I didn't. Maybe I should have realized, but it just didn't occur to me. Have you known for long?'

'Not that long.' The boy relaxed, and Joe suspected that he was glad, in spite of his cool manner, to have got something off his chest. 'Oh, it did occur to me once or twice, when we were younger. But I don't think Jerome himself was really sure, then. Being at boarding school like he was. You know: people go in for that at boarding schools even if they're not really. Public school tradition, isn't it? Burgess and Maclean and so on.'

'So we're told.' Father and son, both products of day schools, looked at each other, both at a loss.

After a minute Joe said: 'I see it clearly now you mention it. I suppose I just didn't pick up the signs because I've known Jerome all his life. I'm sorry, I should have realized sooner. Actually, though you said it gets under Tom's skin I wonder if *they* realize yet? They certainly put on a good act of not knowing.' He recalled Mary, at the beginning of the holiday, joking about the possibilities of Jerome getting off with a chalet girl.

After a moment's thought, David said:

'I think perhaps they do know, but they don't know yet that they do. If you know what I mean?'

'Yes. Yes, I do . . . David?'

'Mmm?' The boy seemed to be brooding.

'I hope – that is, I hope we haven't, by not realizing, ever put you in an embarrassing position? You *or* Jerome – '

'Da-ad,' said David in a world-weary tone, 'are you trying to ask if old Jerome's ever made a pass at me?'

'Well, yes, I do just wonder.'

'Well you can stop wondering. Of couse he hasn't. Dad, honestly – your generation have got one-track minds. Why would he? He knows I'm straight. Most people *are*, and Jerome would be in a right lather if he thought he'd made a false move with anyone he's fond of, you know what he's like. No, he's been mooning over another boy at Oxford for months – he has his photo in his room at home, that's what made me guess and ask as a matter of fact. And just yesterday he got talking to the quiet blond guy who runs the book shop in the big hotel. It was sort of funny, actually, seeing it happen! Lisette and I had to go round the corner to get our faces straight. And afterwards we were teasing Jerome at bit – telling him it'd be a good idea to Come Out with the Non-Scorer – that he wouldn't see that paranoid old Non-Scorer for dust and would have the room to himself.'

Joe felt glad that they could all make a joke of it, suspected that at the deepest level David minded, rather. Jerome: the lifetime's friend, honorary cousin, near brother . . . Another sort of betrayal. But no, on reflection perhaps David would not see it like that, since now he would never lose Jerome.

Joe minded, rather, himself; for Tom, for Mary but mostly for Jerome himself, for the lonely, fraught path the boy would have to tread in the years ahead. He thought of unhandsome but fastidious Jerome frequenting men-only bars, gymnasiums, drag shows or yet more sordid places in the search for others of his own kind: it seemed preposterously out of character. But possibly it was not? A darker image moved beneath the surface: Jerome with the thin, dark thread of masochism that had, on reflection, been there since he was a very small boy, seeking more sinister and equivocal satisfactions: Jerome left lying battered, bleeding and alone on the floor of some squalid room, an ultimate secret place . . . Yet the alternative picture of him in a tasteful apron playing house with another cultured man in a carefully arranged décor was almost equally implausible. Joe intimated this to David, who seemed to ponder a moment before saying reasonably:

'Well he seems likely to go into the theatre, doesn't he? I mean, producing plays is the thing he wants to do. So, in that sort of world, I expect he'll fit in OK.'

'I hadn't thought of that. Perhaps you're right.' From his son's casual wisdom Joe took some small comfort.

'God,' said David suddenly, 'look over there. No, *there* – look!'

The chairs were nearing the foot of the mountain, and on the nursery slope a chain of small but exotic people were stretched out, some hand in hand. Witches in pointed hats and devils with horns, a couple of skeletons, several green-clad creatures of indeterminate sex and one or two disreputable-looking fairies were skiing, linked in a straggling line.

'They're *Fasching* costumes – carnival costumes,' said Joe after a stunned moment. 'But it isn't *Fasching* time. That's later in the winter.'

'It's New Years Eve,' David pointed out.

'So it is. I'd forgotten. Yes, that must be it. Maybe there's a fancy-dress party tonight in the village? . . . But they look like dwarfs.'

David laughed. 'They're *kids*, Dad, can't you see that? They're probably from one of those Austrian school groups that are always pushing ahead in the lift queues. I suppose that man in black's their teacher . . . Don't they look weird, though? Sort of unearthly.'

The wavering line had come to a temporary halt, Silhouetted against the reddening sky. If you were not near enough to see their childish hands, or to hear the chatter and giggles coming from behind the lurid masks and the paint, they looked indeed like an ageless dance of death strung out across the evening-sheened snow. The tall man at their head was the Person in Black himself.

'Ah, I was puzzled to catch sight of you in Baghdad . . . You see, I knew I had an appointment with you in Samarra –'

On Friday afternoon Caroline walked through the village on her way to have a sauna.

She was alone, but not unhappy, imbued with a vague sense of courage and resolution at trying something new. It was the first day of the New Year, bright and still. For the first time in her life she had skipped a lesson, on the pretext that someone should be in the chalet to welcome back Jerome. She was pleased with herself that she managed to dissuade Mary from being that person: it was quite unnecessary for a passionate skier like Mary to waste precious time near the end of the holiday. In consequence, Caroline had spent much of the morning comfortably indoors drinking coffee, first with Pete's knitting wife and then with Jerome, who had been duly delivered back from the hospital in St Wilhelm partly encased in plaster but surprisingly cheerful. Or was it so surprising, on reflection? He had successfully put a stop to his own skiing for this trip, and who knew when he would come again? Perhaps never – for his father, after what had happened, would hardly dare put pressure on him. He had arrogated to himself the rôle of privileged outsider, the bravely uncomplaining invalid to whom everyone must be nice. Clever Jerome. No wonder he was cheerful. Caroline also dared to hope that the shocking scene on the mountain, and the subsequent public row between his parents, had 'cleared the air' a bit in the Lovell family. One heard that scenes sometimes did. Not that she had experience of this herself: rather, it had always seemed to her, that angry words festered, creating secret areas of danger and weakness – but she wanted her friends to be happy together and hoped that perhaps, for them, things worked otherwise.

The only aspect of his present plight that appeared to distress Jerome was the thought of his Mini, now waiting for him, driver-less, at Gatwick.

'Can't your mother drive it home for you? While your father drives their car, I mean.'

'Yes, I suppose she'll have to, though she won't like it. But I was going to drive David and Lisette back to York. If only David had a licence . . .'

'Yes, it's a nuisance he hasn't, isn't it?' said Caroline comfortably. It was a matter of secret relief to her that her son, lacking any prospect of acquiring a car of his own, had not yet shown any great urgency about learning to drive: that was one less perpetual danger to worry about. 'Well, now you can't drive everyone to York,' she said, smiling at Jerome, 'perhaps you'd like to stay with us in London for a few days?'

'May I?'

'Of course.' Her heart lifted. 'Jenn would be awfully pleased to see you too. She's going to come over to supper the day after we get back.' Jenn, although older than Jerome, had shared literary tastes with him when they were children. How lovely if one day Jenn and Jerome . . . But no, no, I mustn't think like that. Things aren't organized like that today, in England. Such a pity.

'That'd be great,' said Jerome fervently, though clearly without any particular reference to Jennifer. 'There's a season of Polish films on at the NFT I'd like to see. I mean, I might as well make good use of the time, as I can't now write the definitive work on Jacobean tragedy I was going to for my tutor.'

'Can't write – ? Oh, of course, your poor arm . . . But it's your *left* arm.'

'But I'm left-handed,' Jerome reminded her, with a beatific smile.

Pete's wife said that it was a proper shame about Jerome's arm, but that he shouldn't expect to be driving again in a hurry. Collarbones took a while to mend, and then he'd need to exercise it carefully to get the muscles working properly; she knew, because Kevin had had a shoulder smashed in a pile-up on the M6 that wasn't his fault and had

161

been off driving for a whole winter – 'And that was really convenient in our line of business, you can imagine.'

'I'm not sure I know what – ?' said Caroline warily.

Pete and Kevin turned out to run a large car-dealing firm just outside Manchester.

'Altringham it is – Cheshire really.'

'Oh yes, I know it. We've got some friends who live in Bowden.' A sudden, clear image of the Morleys' pillared house, lifelike but tiny as in a print, and snow-locked as if it were out here in Austria, came in to her mind. But no, Cheshire, and England, and Anna, were far away: it was probably just wet and grey there. It was much nicer here. After all, she was glad she had come.

'Bowden's quite swish,' said Pete's wife. 'Nice houses. Lot of money there, even these days. Which is just as well for us.'

'Kevin's shoulder's fine now, isn't it?' asked Jerome, with newly acquired concern.

'Well, it doesn't stop him doing anything he wants to,' she replied ambiguously, laughing as usual, showing her white teeth. 'But it does get a bit achey at times, I think. Matter of fact he was complaining about it this morning, and saying he might go for a sauna and massage at the big hotel later in the day, to loosen it up.'

'Oh, I wondered about a sauna,' said Caroline daringly. 'I ache all over today and I've never tried one. Mrs Lovell – that is, Mary – did say yesterday she might be interested, but she and her husband and mine have gone off on a long trek again today and I'm not sure if she'll feel like it when she comes in. I was just wondering if I'd go anyway.'

'Oh well, if you run into Kevin you'll be company for each other,' said Pete's wife laughing her easy laugh. Caroline joined in, assuming it was a joke.

So now she walked, on a perfect winter's day, the length of the quiet, mid-afternoon village, swimsuit rolled in a towel under her arm. Still conscious of its being New Year's day, she walked carefully, savouring the moment, as if it were a space in time between one life and another.

– He was nicer, yesterday. He was so good and competent about Jerome. And then afterwards, when I said to him on the mountain about the children . . . We really seemed to be close, then, for the first time in ages. And then, last night . . . Clutching me to him, sort of violent, so strange, not like he usually is at all, almost as if he were going to cry . . . I'm sore today, but it doesn't really matter, I don't mind. And a swim will be good for me.

In the carpeted, much-draped hall of the hotel, she paid what seemed an enormous number of Austrian schillings to the receptionist and was directed to the 'Health Centre'. It sounded rather austere. But when she reached the pool it was bright azure, shaped irregularly, with curves and shallow steps and fountains, a Disneyland archway and a small copse of tropical plants.

She found the ladies' changing room, noting on the way the sign that said 'To the Sauna'. Two ladies were already dressing or undressing unselfconsciously in the centre of the room, but Caroline retreated to one of the side-cubicles and drew the curtains. At the girls' boarding school where she had been a pupil from twelve to eighteen, it had not been the done thing to appear naked; one always put one's knickers on, for instance, before removing one's nightdress. Caroline had never got into the habit of stripping unconcernedly, even in front of Jennifer. Nor had she ever come to consider her own body, when unprotected and adorned, attractive. Part of her wariness about having a sauna was that she was not quite sure what the form was and if the other women in it would wear swim suits or not. Well anyway, she told herself, that was their business; she could always wear hers. Meanwhile, though she was a poor swimmer, she meant to enjoy her dip in the ridiculous artificial paradise.

She did enjoy it, discovering a bubbling jacuzzi area, and began to wish she had the children with her. Perhaps they could all come for a final family treat tomorrow, before Joe got his night train to Vienna? But no, he would want to ski till the light faded, and then he would have to change and pack and eat something, there would hardly be time. Well it would be fun to run into someone she knew now. Kevin would do.

Finally she made herself leave the pool, promising herself another swim to cool off after the sauna ritual. Wasn't that what one did? She followed signs for the sauna and reached a semi-lit antechamber with lounging chairs and piles of thick towels. (She need not, she realized now, have troubled to bring her own towel. This luxurious place was all so different from the dank, echoing, chlorine-tainted public pools to which she had dutifully escorted the children when they were small.) One chair contained a huddled, towel-swathed form. Perhaps one might even have a nap oneself, afterwards. She saw the wooden cabin that was clearly the sauna, and pulled open the door. A burst of heat met her. She stepped forward bracing herself for it – and then stepped back hastily, gasping:

'Oh – I'm so sorry – '

On the slatted seats facing her, in varying postures of recumbent unconcern were several men, all of them completely naked.

She shut the door on them again and lent against the outside of it, burning not with the blast of heat she had encountered but with embarrassment. How could she have made such a mistake? It must say 'Gents', or rather '*Herren*' somewhere, and she had simply failed to notice. But she had been so sure – and had seen no notice saying '*Damen*' either, except in the far changing room.

The cabin door opened again, and she jumped and moved away from it. But it was a woman who came out, naked herself except for a towel skimpily draped round her matronly hips. Caroline must have failed to see her inside, in the reddish half-light of the cabin.

'You go in?' asked the woman with bossy, Germanic kindness. 'There is place.' She held the door open for Caroline. And Caroline found herself going in.

Evidently, she realized in whirling confusion as she averted her eyes and subsided onto a low bench to one side, she had failed to understand several things about present-day life, and among them was the fact that the remark about Kevin being company for her had been no arch joke but a simple statement of fact.

And indeed, when she dared raise her eyes above her own white, bony knees, one of her several companions proved to be Kevin, reclining hairily on a higher shelf opposite her.

'Hallo,' she said almost inaudibly, thinking how indecent he looked.

'Ah, I thought it was you,' he replied heartily, and added after a minute, with the air of a host making polite conversation: 'Hot enough for you?'

'Oh yes, thank you,' she said, thinking, My God, it's *boiling*. I'm not staying here long, for that reason – as well as any other . . . But one of the other men said:

'Well, I'm going to add a bit more water to the brazier, if none of you mind,' and he got down to do so. A paunchy, middle-aged figure, he moved unconcernedly. She saw him silhouetted, chest, thickened waist, genitals, against the glow of brazier as he sprinkled pine-scented water onto it from a pot with a ladle, like a figure in some medieval painting of hell. A cloud of heady steam arose and he drew back, covering his face, and then looked round at the others, smiling in apology. His face was reddened by the mountain sun; the rest of him was white as if always buried, summer as well as winter, under layers of clothes. She thought: he looks harmless. Not a young man. Older than Joe, in fact. And not an educated voice. But just – pleasant and natural. Maybe it isn't so bad in here. Maybe I can stand it for a few minutes after all.

She closed her eyes for a minute to try to compose herself. Kevin, and another man on the ledge above her who sounded young, started a desultory conversation about steel erection. For a moment, with a resurgence of defensiveness, she morbidly wondered if this could be an obscene joke directed at herself, as the only woman at the moment present. But no – their voices were quite casual, and anyway the atmosphere wasn't like that. She began to relax again.

The conversation settled onto oil rigs and the problems of maintaining them out at sea. The middle-aged man joined in, and it became apparent that he and the unseen younger man both worked with an oil company off Aberdeen. What unlikely people not only went skiing these days but stayed in the best hotels, thought Caroline idly – and then thought: for heaven's sake, my girl, you sound like your mother! It isn't in the least unlikely; people are very well paid on oil rigs. 'You're prudish *and* snobbish,' she told herself severely, like Alice in Wonderland, but the very fact of formulating the thought cheered her rather than depressed her: she must be making progress. And the conversation was actually quite interesting, in a mild, male way. She thought she remembered Jane Austen saying that she never put male conversation into her books because she did not know what men talked about on their own, and then imagined Jane Austen sitting here in the sauna and giggled inwardly. She had never expected to feel one-up on Jane Austen, but really . . .

She was beginning to sweat. She stole a look at Kevin, lying opposite, and saw that he was now damp and glistening like a seal. What funny things human bodies were, such variety within the basic form. The younger man, muttering about heat up top, came down to a lower ledge where she could see him. He was spare and well built: he reminded her of David. Kevin and the older man looked gross, but their faces were nice, and ordinary, and she remembered how well Kevin had played the piano the other evening. After all, perhaps nakedness wasn't so much ugly and a little ridiculous, as she had thought, but just vulnerable and somehow touching in its very explicitness.

Sweat ran down her breasts inside her decent, one-piece swimsuit. She suddenly felt horribly constricted and – yes – worse than constricted: she felt foolish. Wasn't it a little *rude* (really, no other word) to sit encased in elasticized nylon when no one else was? On a sudden decision, she undid the straps and removed it.

'You'll be more comfortable like that,' said Kevin, patronizing but kind.

166

The younger man went off to swim. She was a little sorry, because she had been getting interested in the problems of putting up drilling rigs in the North Sea. So when the older man, who seemed to enjoy talking, turned to her and said he hoped they hadn't been boring her – extreme politeness was the convention, she noted, in this otherwise unconventional situation – she said not at all, and perhaps he could tell her how ski lifts were put up in inaccessible bits of mountain, because she had sometimes wondered?

So, for the next fifteen minutes, he told her just how it was done (with helicopter loads of concrete and a great deal of money) until at last she had to interrupt and say, 'I'm most terribly sorry, I *must* go out of here for a bit or I shall explode with heat.'

'Oh, I do apologize, I should have thought,' he said contritely – he really was a nice man – 'Yes, you pop straight into the shower opposite. You'll get palpitations if you stay in here overtime. I'm about at that point myself.'

She walked unconcernedly to the shower carrying her swimsuit and sluiced away the sweat. She let the water pour over her head too, though in the pool earlier she had worn her usual rubber bathing cap. She thought, in miniature revelation: why bother with a cap – ever again? So, one's hair gets wet. So, one can dry it. Young girls never seem to wear caps these days, and their hair looks just as nice.

When she came out of the shower her friend of the oil rigs was just emerging from the sauna cabin.

'I think I'll have another swim before I go,' she said happily. 'Shall you?'

'No – if you'll excuse me, I'm a bit tired now. I had a long swim before. Er – ' he smiled at her, 'Don't forget to put your costume on again before you go in the pool!'

'Goodness – Thank you: I nearly had forgotten! One gets so used to being like this . . .'

'I know. That's why I reminded you. Tell you what, before I shower I'm going to have a bit of a snooze here. Do you think you could put a couple of towels over me when I'm laying down, there's a kind girl?'

'Of course I will,' she said.

He extended himself fleshily, like a giant baby, on one of the loungers. As if he had been one of her own small children, she tucked two large, soft towels round him. He sighed with pleasure. She had a sudden impulse to bestow a kiss upon his coarsened cheek, but perhaps better not . . .

'I'm off for my swim,' she said brightly, and went.

Outside, the night and stars had come. Feeling extraordinarily clean, as if washed without and within, she mounted the village street, enjoying the frosty air on her face as a continuation of the physical experience of the last two hours. Not a trace of soreness now, in spite of last night. How good. Oh, perhaps the turn of the year *has* brought a change of fortune, perhaps everything . . . us . . . everything . . . is going to be all right after all?

I wonder if Jerome's accident somehow changed the mixture, made Joe think – ? No, it was before that, I believe . . . Did something happen to him on the mountain, during that snow storm the day before yesterday? Something that frightened him – sort of shook him into a new mood? Not so hostile. I can't ask him. But I believe it did.

I won't ever ask him. I'll just go on, quietly, hoping for the best. Yes, that is my rôle, what I have to do, my own strength. What I am there for.

The level crossing gates were shut, a bell ringing in the night. It sounded sad and Middle European, like a scene in a film about the war. She waited, in company with a few other people, and presently a long, dark train pulled away from the station and trundled past, gathering speed. Compagnie des Wagons-Lits compartments slid past, and it occurred to her that this was the evening express, the night train to Vienna. This time tomorrow Joe would be on it. She suppressed an obscure pain. But it's all right, Joe. You'll come back, and I'll be there at home, and we'll go on. You needn't worry. I won't give up on you – us . . . And I suppose I might even learn to be a bit different myself. Just a bit. Less what the children call Mummyish, perhaps. Less nervous and fussy.

Making things better . . . It isn't impossible. Life lasts such a long time. Tomorrow is the first day of the rest of my life.

She left the gaunt railway-lines behind, and trudged happily up to the snowy side path that led to the chalet, towards the lit but curtained windows, towards the hidden future.

On Saturday night the train left with Joe on board. Imbued with the riotous regret of holiday-ending, the entire Beech-Lovell clan, even Jerome with his plastered arm and shoulder, had been at the station to see Joe off. The next day they would fly to London.

>   . . . *Simple goodbyes to children and friends become*
> *A felon's numb*
> *Farewell.*

But tonight the poem that had haunted his journey did not mean much to him. For once he felt insulated from this goodbye, as if it had already taken place. As if it were a physical ritual, warm but without the power to move; like sex without emotional involvement. He hugged David with one arm – regretting a little in passing, as always, that his English son would not embrace him as a European son would have done, but that was all old history now: David, cheerful, friendly, defensive, so close, so alien, was as he was. Joe embraced Lisette, and only here felt a tremor of apprehension, a hint of his old, nameless pain. *Let her stay with David, not be hurt, not leave us . . .*

'Come down from York again with David one weekend soon, won't you, lovey?'

She nodded eagerly, without speaking, glowing, her sunburnt skin momentarily against his. Then Caroline. And then they were all separated from him, Lisette, David, Jerome, Mary, Tom, Caroline – all just faces, coloured by the mountain sun and wind and snow, whitened again by the sulphurous light of the station lamps, looking up at him in a semicircle as he stood out of reach on the carriage steps. And then he stepped back and the doors swung shut, and then the train was moving, and then they were gone, and the station was gone and the level crossing and the lights of the outlying houses, and Heiligenhof was gone, and he was alone at last and on his final way.

He found his seat and made himself look through a book in German about a scientific renaissance in the court of Elizabeth of Bohemia, which his firm was thinking of publishing, and whose scholarly author he was due to see on Tuesday.

The others in his compartment, who would be his companions during the crowded night in couchettes, looked like business men: two of then conversed intermittently in Dutch or Flemish, passing papers to one another. The one woman, elderly, sallow, in furs, seemed a typical Viennese returning home after some family New Year in Switzerland or Germany. When considerably later in the evening, he went down the swaying, repetitive corridors in search of a beer and a sandwich, it came as a slight surprise to find that on this train there were still skiers here and there: Austrians, anachronistic in bright, padded clothes, homeward-bound but talking with the loud cheerfulness of the open air, encumbering the end of the coaches with their gear. His own gear he had left with his family to take back to England, and this night train, sealed against the outside air, seemed to be moving through another dimension than the one in which he had existed for the last seven days.

He was travelling onwards, onwards, with only brief stops at unseen stations where lonely loudspeakers garbled German into the dark, and no one in his part of the train left or came: onwards and eastwards for a whole night across the length of Austria, itself the 'Eastland', as if the heavy train was set to penetrate the iron curtain and beyond, into the hinterlands of the old Empire across the great Hungarian plain, into the one-time Ottoman lands, into Asia itself. But then even

Vienna was well to the east by European standards: farther east than Berlin or Prague, a part of the West today only by the vagaries of recent history: only after Stalin's death had the whole of Austria been dragged westwards, and chance might so easily have taken it the other way. It nearly did once before. The Turks had got right to the walls of the Old City: Aunt Sophie's address in Turkenschanzplatz testified to their presence. *'Asien fängt an der Landstrasse an'*: 'Asia begins at the Landstrasse' . . . All that coffee, and Persian carpeting used to cover sofa and tables in a way it never was in cities further west. Not to mention the Middle Eastern race that had made Vienna their own city.

Yet against this sense of travelling far through the night to an essentially exotic place was the persistent, submerged idea of journeying backwards; not only in space but also in time, back to some sheltered, zero-place, some warm, shuttered, half-remembered room with high furniture, a hidden place, a secret one – *safety*, at last.

On that train he felt safe, and very happy.

And tomorrow – unless something went wrong – there would be Anna. But it was almost as if that were an extra bonus, not the central reason for his happiness but something he only remembered now, like a man waking from a confused sleep, as additional reason for pleasure.

When he returned to his compartment the attendant had been round lowering the berths. In the small floor space the other occupants were shuffling off their shoes, looking vainly for somewhere to stow their coats, getting in each others' way. He retreated to his top bunk, taking his duffel bag up with him. He had not taken his Notebook out for several days, but now he leafed through it. It was nearly full.

When it is full, he thought, with something like a small surge of relief, then perhaps it will be time to stop keeping it. Perhaps, then, some pattern will have emerged in it. Or perhaps, simply, it will have served its purpose, and I won't need to read what's in it any more. Finished. Over. Like the period of time it represents. After all, I am not a writer. However much I may think I have something to say, I cannot create other lives. I have only my own life through which to express myself.

Ted Litvak says – used to say – that, in any case, novels and stories constitute by their very form, a fundamental distortion of truth. They cannot help imposing on the fluidity of reality an artificial shape: the reader sees when he is at the beginning, or in the middle, or, most of all, when he is nearing the end. He feels the flimsiness of the last few pages, running out between his fingers like sands in an hourglass, and sees that the book is about to breathe its last. Something finite is about to occur, a death (if only metaphorically) at any rate a removal. Inevitably that affects his whole perception of what is happening in the book, and writers, knowing this, use the fact to play tricks. Furthermore – Ted was particularly insistent on this point, and as he was a storyteller himself he had a right to be – on account of its sheer physical form, *any* novel, however apparently realistic, is a box of tricks. Because it imitates the lineal nature of time, commonly recounting events in the order in which they occur, it makes the reader believe that it is an adequate representation of time lived. But it is not, because time is lived on a moving frontier, with what lies behind clear but what lies ahead always invisible; whereas time in a story is really all past time, all palpably there, down to the last page and the last word, before the reader even embarks. It's a con, Ted used to say, in his rich, ineradicable German accent. It is a con, my boy.

But I think it cons writers themselves in return. Look at Mary, letting on the other day that she thinks the future is always already there. Of course, she is a writer, she sees life in terms of stories: how else can she see it?

For some, a book with pages all inexorably there, even if uncut. For me – a landscape. All there too, even if hidden from view. For Anna? . . . I don't know. How strange. I really do not know how Anna envisages the future. In the banal sense of those words, we have always avoided talking about the future, for several reasons, but I believe that in a deeper sense *she really does not think the future is there*. Perhaps

172

that is one of the things about her that make her seem, in spite of everything that has happened or failed to happen to her, in some way invulnerable. She does not count on anything, so she does not dread either. Oh Anna. Free Anna. Will I really see you tomorrow? What a long journey this has been.

He reread the passage about the lemmings he had copied out on his last evening in London. Poor little buggers, convinced they were setting out for some magic land, when all the time . . . They have a vision of the future, in their own furry way. Trouble is, they've got it wrong. Like Uncle Sigi, setting off for America, hoping for a new life there.

Only when he lay in his bunk under the old-fashioned blanket-bag that the Compagnie des Wagons-Lits provided, did he recollect that there was one piece of the immediate future that he did know, though it would happen far from him: tomorrow Ted Litvak would be laid in the sodden winter earth of a cemetary to the north of London. Now he found himself wishing he had thought to ask Naomi the time of the ceremony, because he would like to call into a synagogue at that hour, as some kind of gesture of – of what? Not prayer, no, he had no prayers, but perhaps of sheer remembrance for Ted, recognition, in Ted's own city. Always supposing he could find a synagogue in Vienna: it occurred to him that he had no idea where one might be.

I could ring Naomi tomorrow morning and ask her what time –

No. No, better not. It would simply remind her of my absence, my defection. Not there is not there: I will make no sign to anyone in England till I come back.

I can find a synagogue and sit there a while anyway. The exact hour doesn't signify. There'll surely be one, or several, even today, in that rag-trade area off Mariahilferstrasse. The tram from the Westbahnhof to the Old City goes down Mariahilferstrasse anyway: I'll keep my eyes open. No, it'll be dark then, still. I'll come back later in the morning. I've got most of the day, in fact. Anna said she probably wouldn't be arriving till the afternoon, she wasn't sure what time or where she'd be coming from, and then she has to get in from the airport. She never wants me to meet her at an airport or station, for some reason. She'd rather just find me, at whatever hotel we've agreed on. Or I find her, waiting in our locked room, reading or showering or brushing her hair, our separate and secret life already begun, as if it has been going on there all the time and I – and she – have simply regained it once more.

He lay under the creaking compartment roof, with the insistent noise of the wheels on the rails and his hand over his quietly beating heart, and gave himself up at last to long thoughts of Anna. He lay thus for much of the night. Time passed, and he was not awake but not fully asleep either. Untouched for once by rueful memories of the past or by yearning hopes and fears for the future, he lay in a kind of quiet ecstasy, moving from reverie into fleeting dreams and then back into waking thoughts again. It seemed to him one of the longest nights of his life and yet one of the most precious: he wanted it never to end. Yet some time in the very early morning he slipped into deeper sleep; Anna moved soundless from him – perhaps to sleep herself – and when he and the rest of the carriage were jerked into wakefulness by the attendant's baton rattling down the doors, he found himself alone again.

The 58 tram trundled through a Sunday morning Vienna wrapped in a winter darkness that only lingeringly gave way to a grey day. Joe, with his duffel bag and a brief case, got off at the Ringstrasse. He would walk the rest of the way to the hotel, somewhere the far side of Stefansdom. He crossed the Burggarten, which lay petrified under a layer of frost, and thought of making a short detour to the Opera House, looming ghostly beyond the trees, to see what was on and if he could get some seats for Anna and himself for later in the week. But no, the ticket office would not be open yet, and anyway he was cold, now, and needed coffee, a shower, a shave. He was not tired: the elation that had kept him between waking and sleeping in the night was still with him, but Vienna seemed to be half-hiding from him. It was indeed as if he had arrived at a theatre too early, and the set was still partly under dustsheets, with only a few desultory stagehands beginning to set out the movable pieces: the wrought iron work, the lacy winter branches, the stone people. He would have to contain himself, waiting patiently for the action to begin.

He turned into the narrow Neuer Markt, and then into Kartnerstrasse, bedecked with Christmas trees. Here in the Old City the stagehands were beginning to light and sweep the coffee shops. A physical pleasure invaded him at the thought of the coffee and Viennese rolls – or perhaps onion soup? – that he would presently consume, but he decided to postpone this pleasure also to go on enjoying it in anticipation.

In the heart of the city, in the swept and garnished expanse of the new pedestrian area, Stefansdom was pealing a Sunday tone. The main doors of the cathedral were open, light and warmth streamed out, and a trickle of people were going in, gloved and fur-hatted for the first mass of the day. Again, Joe was tempted to stop and join them for a few minutes, perhaps even to add a private candle for Ted to the golden haze of candles that stood by the baroque shrines. But this great church was not Ted's place, nor his, and anyway he had his luggage . . . Again, he pressed on.

At the comfortably old-fashioned hotel hidden down an alley off Bäckerstrasse, he was told his room was ready and there was a telephone message for him. He took the folded paper with a tightening of both joy and foreboding in his breast, thinking: Anna. Anna had never failed him – badly – yet, but there was always the possibility, something beyond her control . . . Or she might simply be reassuring him, 'I'm coming'.

But the message was from his opposite number, the editor-in-chief at a Viennese publishing house, politely welcoming him and confirming that they had a lunch appointment on Monday.

Following the elderly porter up the wide, wooden staircase, he conquered his disappointment by telling himself that, after all, no news was good news. She *must* be coming, if she didn't say she wasn't.

Not till he was upstairs, washing the night journey away under a hot but temperamental shower, did it occur to him that the message might conceivably have turned out to be something quite other, an urgent summons home, for instance. That simply hadn't crossed his mind. He let the inappropriate, intruding thought fall away from him.

Dressed again, he felt slightly light-headed, but very clean. The feather quilt on the bed was a white, puffed mound. He thought that perhaps he should have a nap there later in the day, and then when he woke the early winter dark would be coming down again over the lace-curtained windows and soon Anna, Anna . . . But the happiness of repose, too, he left in store, and went out again, restless and eager, into the brightening cold.

He went back to the cathedral square and ordered his breakfast at a big café on the corner of the Graben, but when it came he realized he was not hungry for rolls, and even the coffee, a *grosser Bräuner*, suddenly seemed too rich and strong, inducing in him a heady feeling that was near to sickness. *Grosser Bräuner* and *Kleiner Schwarzer*: the ubiquitous café phrases had always sounded like the names of fairytale characters to him anyway. *Fasching* hobgoblins, they swam up from his earliest childhood, grotesque but reassuring because unchanging. Like the waiters' black jackets and long white aprons, like the heavy, good quality overcoats and traditional hats worn by passers-by, both men and women, or like the *Wienerisch* dialect he heard on people's lips: these things were of all time. Safe, safe – in spite of everything. In this city, more than anywhere, he could lay down his head.

But, as if aware that an incipient exhaustion threatened him, he was possessed by the desire to act, to walk, to look, before it should strike him down. To find, even. But find what? For the moment, he could not quite remember.

He walked back across the Old City, along Rotenturm-strasse, past Ruprechtkirche, and down the high steps at the bottom to the quay of the Danube canal. He had known he had some reason for going through the old Jewish quarter but only now, inadvertently passing the site of the Gestapo house, did he remember what: he needed to look for a synagogue. Yes. But why? For Anna, the other Anna, who here, here . . . No. No, that wasn't it. He needed to find a synagogue for his father. No – for Ted.

Plenty of time for that later in the morning. The icy breath of the petrified canal touched his eyes, his lips. He looked up and down it. Away to the right the giant Ferris wheel in the Prater stood skeletal above the sweep of buildings. He hesitated a moment more, and then set out across a bridge in search of it.

He half expected the fairground to be shut at this season, but, perhaps because it was just after Christmas and the New Year, or perhaps simply because it was Sunday, quite a few of the stalls were open or opening. Electric lights hung in jewelled necklaces in the grey air. There was a smell of wood from burning braziers, of chestnuts and frying potatoes and cocoanut ice and fresh dough. Hatted men in dirty sheepskin coats were setting up shooting galleries, women fat as peasant dolls with layers of clothing under their overcoats, were laying out toys and jewellery and baubles of Bohemian glass. His step quickened, till at last he reached the foot of the great wheel.

'Möchte der Herr auf dem Riesenrad fahren?'

'I might – will it start soon?'

'If the very noble gentelman will take his seat,' continued the attendant in stately German, but with a hint of malicious-ness in his eyes: 'then the Wheel shall start.' Joe climbed into one of the covered cabins, rather sceptical, prepared himself for a chilly delay but evidently the attendant had been waiting to gather a sufficient sprinkling of people onto the wheel, for it soon started.

Up they rose, and Joe found himself back in a ski lift and gazing out across a toy spread for his entertainment. Like the uncaring bird whose view had become the city's classic panorama, his revolving eye swept the enormous, minature, grey-brown Vienna spread at his feet: canal and boulevards and rooftops, domes and spires, the green-grey patches of the Stadtpark and the Belvedere and more distant gardens, the tight-packed centre (Bäckerstrasse hidden in its heart), the railway lines, the Danube, the motorways, Stefansdom, Karlskirche, the Votirkirche behind which his birthplace had been, Berggasse, the vast Allgemeine Krankenhaus where Freud worked, and a million matchboxes of the outer districts stretching to meet the snow-speckled hills of the Wienerwald. Like time past, present and to come, it lay spread out below him, his landscape of love and death from which he was nevertheless, ultimately and always, an outsider. And here indeed he was, separated from it, suspended in the air above it like a disembodied spirit, cut off from human reality. '*Up into an high place . . .*' Only now he remembered the scene in *The Third Man*, where one man (the Devil, surely?) takes another up on this same wheel, shows him the human beings walking like insects far, far below, and says, 'Would you really care if one of these were wiped out?'

Now, taking his eyes from the distant hills, he peered over the edge, directly down – and there, indeed, were the insects, infinitely remote.

Dizziness came over him. For a moment he almost thought: *So this is it. I am going to fall. After all, this is it.* But the Viennese, perhaps in awareness of their own predilection for such fatal events, had constructed and glazed the cabins solidly: even a man feeling faint and sick could not easily fling himself out. He drew some deep breaths – and found himself still upright, clutching a bar, with the wheel descending again.

It was then, near the ground, that he saw a familiar figure. In a long overcoat and an old-fashioned Homburg hat, such as men still wore in this city, he was making his way slowly up a path. Joe did not see his face, but he recognized his walk.

178

With his usual quick reaction to any unexpected event, Joe shouted to the attendant to stop the wheel at the moment when his cabin reached the bottom – he wanted to get out.

Obedient as a ski lift in an emergency, the wheel stopped. 'Sir doesn't seem to have given himself much time to enjoy his ride,' the attendant said sarcastically, as Joe scrambled past him with a muttered apology. Through the turnstiles, round to the other side to find the path up which the figure had been walking: only a minute or so had been lost – He set off at a trot up the path, branched off onto another, hesitated, ran back the way he had come. Then he began to search more randomly among the stalls of the funfair that were like a market in an eastern city; up and down the lanes he went, hope declining, but still half believing that round a corner of a booth would come the known face, or he would catch sight of a familiar turn of the head . . . Gradually he slowed to a walk, and then stopped.

Of course it would not happen – could not happen. It simply was not possible.

He must have had some momentary fit of delusion, as well as giddiness, up there on the wheel. Just as well he had come down. He had better stay on the ground now, with the rest of the human race.

He had also, he told himself, better get an hour or two's sleep to put himself right before Anna came. But first there was the other thing he had to find. A small mission to accomplish that now, more than ever, seemed important.

He decided to get the U–Bahn back under the canal and the Old City, to Karlsplatz.

At the end of the morning he was wandering in the Mariahilf district.

It occurred to him that this was probably where his true roots lay. Not in the medieval ghetto of Rotenturmstrasse, nor yet, really, in the Ringstrasse and the streets behind the Votirkirche where his socially conscious parents had set up their home, but in the nineteenth-century clothing district where his grandfathers had had their workshops, their accumulating, hoarded wealth, their being, and where he now walked as a stranger.

There were old houses between Mariahilferstrasse and Gumpendorferstrasse that must have been there before the Ringstrasse was laid out, when walls separated the City from these outlying parts and Gumperdorferstrasse itself petered out into fields and market gardens. These enormous houses stretched through from one main street to another via a chain of inner courtyards and arched passageways. Distracted from his search for a synagogue, he explored a couple of labyrinthine dwellings. There were battered notices advertizing for tailoring hands and packers, but they looked as if they might be out of date. The damps and chills of more than a hundred winters bloomed on the darkened stones. In the cobbled corners of the inner courtyards lay heaps of congealed, unmelting snow.

He wanted to penetrate the old staircases, into the rooms deep within the houses, to find there great, lumpy, lace-covered beds, streaked velvet hangings, worn Persian carpets, tarnished silver *menorahs*, forgotten wallpapers, secret places. But all, this morning, seemed to be locked, deserted.

He caught sight of another notice, enamelled. It said 'Sieger Couture' and he laughed aloud at the happy omen, and thought that he would bring Anna here, tomorrow or the next day, to see her own name. Four whole days they would have, most of the time together. A lifetime.

He emerged onto a street he did not recognize, and walked up it in the direction where (he had been told) a synagogue lay, seeking a landmark. To his vague surprise, he found himself once again nearing the Westbahnhof. He must have taken a wrong turning.

The brief brightness of the morning was over. The skies had lowered themselves again and now a thin sleet began to fall, a delicate tracery against the heavy buildings. The metal rails made long, silver streaks in the roadway where the one-eyed trams passed.

Suddenly, feeling overcome with exhaustion at last, he

forgot his mission and decided to take another 58 tram home, back to the Old City.

Crossing the complex junction and ring road in front of the station, he lost his bearings again and hesitated. No, he couldn't go home yet. He had something else to do. But what?

He saw what seemed to be the main tram-stop across an expanse of roadway. Some trams were stationary there; rails led away in various directions. Some cars were drawn up at lights a little way away, but the road immediately in front was clear.

It was then that he saw Ted Litvak. This time, he could not believe he was mistaken. Ted, wearing an Austrian hat and an old loden jacket, was just boarding a tram. He saw the face clearly in profile. There was not a moment to lose. The lights were changing. He ran out across the empty space, calling Ted's name.

Then it happened. A great, single eye was suddenly dazzling him: he veered away from it, and into the hot roar of a car radiator grid he called again, desperately, Ted's name. But perhaps he only thought he called it, for the air itself seemed to snatch his voice from him, carrying it off vertiginously to a great distance. Something had hit him hard, and then he was falling, falling far down from the Prater wheel, spinning across the skies above Vienna, down, down from the lift over the silent white precipice, down past the rocks and bridges over nothing, down into the great, grey, unreflecting pool, down into the dark.

Down into death, or life. A new life beyond the abyss, or a no-life, annihilation or discovery, into emptiness or a great light, which was itself a warm, well-lighted place or an endless snow. Or just a version of tomorrow –

Or another room entirely.